"So..." *Erin asked casually,*
turning on her tape recorder.
"What's *your idea of the perfect date?"*

Jared paused. "A leisurely drive to the coast.
We'd walk on the beach and have lunch at some
cute little place, maybe buy saltwater taffy and
fresh-baked bread. Then we'd walk through
town and stop at the bumper cars, go for a spin
on the merry-go-round, feed the sea lions at the
aquarium. Later we'd find some nice, out-of-the-
way seafood restaurant and have clam chowder,
garlic bread, whatever else strikes our fancy. After
dinner, we'd drive home, exhausted and fat, but
happy."

Erin sat as still as stone, stunned by what he'd
said. If he'd read her mind, he couldn't have
picked a more perfect response. The only thing
she might add would be a long night at a cozy
little bed-and-breakfast. Provided, of course, that
her date was *Jared....*

Dear Reader,

We've been busy here at Silhouette Romance cooking up the next batch of tender, emotion-filled romances to add extra sizzle to your day.

First on the menu is Laurey Bright's modern-day Sleeping Beauty story, *With His Kiss* (#1660). Next, Melissa McClone whips up a sensuous, *Survivor*-like tale when total opposites must survive two weeks on an island, in *The Wedding Adventure* (#1661). Then bite into the next juicy SOULMATES series addition, *The Knight's Kiss* (#1663) by Nicole Burnham, about a cursed knight and the modern-day princess who has the power to unlock his hardened heart.

We hope you have room for more, because we have three other treats in store for you. First, popular Silhouette Romance author Susan Meier turns on the heat in *The Nanny Solution* (#1662), the third in her DAYCARE DADS miniseries about single fathers who learn the ABCs of love. Then, in Jill Limber's *Captivating a Cowboy* (#1664), are a city girl and a dyed-in-the-wool cowboy a recipe for disaster...or romance? Finally, Lissa Manley dishes out the laughs with *The Bachelor Chronicles* (#1665), in which a sassy journalist is assigned to get the city's most eligible—and stubborn—bachelor to go on a blind date!

I guarantee these heartwarming stories will keep you satisfied until next month when we serve up our list of great summer reads.

Happy reading!

Mary-Theresa Hussey

Mary-Theresa Hussey
Senior Editor

Please address questions and book requests to:
Silhouette Reader Service
U.S.: 3010 Walden Ave., P.O. Box 1325, Buffalo, NY 14269
Canadian: P.O. Box 609, Fort Erie, Ont. L2A 5X3

The Bachelor Chronicles

LISSA MANLEY

SILHOUETTE *Romance*®

Published by Silhouette Books

America's Publisher of Contemporary Romance

For Kevin, Laura and Sean, for being so patient and self-sufficient while I write. Your faith and support means the world to me. I love you all.

Special thanks to my incredibly gifted critique group Leah Vroman, Terri Reed and Delilah Ahrendt. I couldn't have done this without you. You guys are the best.

 SILHOUETTE BOOKS

ISBN 0-373-19665-2

THE BACHELOR CHRONICLES

Visit Silhouette at www.eHarlequin.com

Printed in U.S.A.

LISSA MANLEY

has been an avid reader of romance since her teens and firmly believes that writing romances with happy endings is her dream job. She lives in the beautiful Pacific Northwest with her college-sweetheart husband of nineteen years, Kevin, two children, Laura and Sean, and two feisty toy poodles named Lexi and Angel, who run the household and get away with it. She has a degree in business from the University of Oregon, having discovered the joys of writing well after her college years. In her spare time, she enjoys reading, crafting, attending her children's sporting events, and relaxing at the family vacation home on the Oregon coast.

Lissa loves to hear from her readers. She can be reached at P.O. Box 91336, Portland, OR 97291-0336, or at http://lissamanley.com.

MEMO

To: Erin James, Staff Reporter
From: Joe Capriati, Assignment Editor
Subject: THE BACHELOR CHRONICLES

Erin—

The Beacon will be running a special-interest feature entitled THE BACHELOR CHRONICLES, which will consist of interviews with local, wealthy bachelors.

To motivate a little healthy competitive reporting, the reporter who turns in the most interesting, attention-grabbing piece will win the byline, a nice bonus and will write the follow-up I have planned.

This is a great opportunity for you, Erin. Find an interesting bachelor (or two) and write a juicy story. Maybe this will be the big break you've been after for the last year.

Get out there and snag a fantastic man!

Chapter One

Erin James stepped into Warfield's, the hottest java bar in Portland, Oregon, and inhaled deeply, savoring the rich scent of freshly ground coffee. She adjusted her glasses, and her gaze landed on the guy standing behind the counter, studded-out in a designer suit, gold chains and enough hair grease to roast a pig. He had to be Jared Warfield. No surprise that he looked like a carbon copy of every other bachelor she'd interviewed in the past week for her article.

She moved toward the counter and mentally cursed "The Bachelor Chronicles," her latest project. Interviewing rich bachelors who reminded her way too much of her heartless ex-husband, Brent, seemed trivial. But her editor had promised a fat bonus to the reporter who came up with the best story, and she was counting on getting the byline.

She hated the story idea, which involved featuring wealthy local bachelors in the *Beacon* and then having each bachelor go on a date with one of the women who wrote to the paper. But she would interview Frankenstein if it kept her house out of foreclosure, the wonderful legacy her ex had bestowed upon her when he'd lost his gigantic trust fund in day trading two years ago, then taken off to parts unknown with one of Erin's best friends. She'd been stuck with his overdue credit card debt and a mortgage payment she hadn't been able to cover in months. For the millionth time, Erin wished she'd had the brains to close out their joint charge account before their divorce had been final a year ago.

A pang of anxiety slid through her. She knew too well where uncontrollable spending could land a person. She had no intention of repeating her mother's mistakes or of hanging on the hairy brink of homelessness. Never again.

Frowning, she pressed a hand to her midsection, systematically forcing herself to relax. She would be a fool to alienate Jared Warfield with a sour attitude before she could get the interview that could turn her life around.

Taking several deep breaths, she manufactured her best reporter smile, determined to free herself from the financial mess she'd been left in and make a new start, on her own.

"May I help you?" Mr. Oily Hair said.

"Yes, Mr. Warfield. I'm Erin James from the *Beacon*." She extended her hand over the counter.

He shook her hand. "It's very nice to meet you, Ms. James, but I'm Dan Swopes, the manager. This is Mr. Warfield." He gestured to the man who had just walked behind the counter, a tray of dirty coffee cups in his hands.

Erin barely kept her jaw from falling. *That* was Jared Warfield, maverick entrepreneur, casually dressed in beige khakis and a navy-blue polo shirt? He looked more like the cashier than the millionaire owner of one of the fastest growing businesses in the city.

As Erin struggled to shift gears, her feminine interest exploded. Jared Warfield was good-looking—very good-looking—in an unconventional kind of way. His buzz-cut dark hair, while severe, enhanced the chiseled bone structure of his face. His mouth was generous yet masculine, and his eyes, which he turned toward her as she stepped closer, were the most unusual shade of brown she'd ever seen. They reminded her of the steaming coffee in mugs being handed over the counter. Rich, dark, yummy coffee.

His well-fitting, short-sleeved shirt accentuated a toned chest, broad, capable shoulders, nicely muscled arms and a taut waist. He was tall and lean and hot, and on second look, much too self-assured and imposing to be the cashier.

Her heart spasmed in her chest and she faltered, but quickly recovered, chiding herself as she moved toward the register. She wasn't about to have a heart attack over the first really handsome man she'd encountered since her divorce. Brent had been just as gorgeous on the outside, but as ugly as a worm-filled, rotten apple on the inside. Appearances, she'd discovered, were very deceiving.

She took a deep breath and smiled politely. "Oh, I see I've made a mistake." She extended her hand. "Erin James, Mr. Warfield."

He put the tray down, wiped his hands on a towel and reached out and shook her hand. "Ms. James," he said, pressing his lips together in a strange scowl. "I'll finish up here, and then we can sit down and have some coffee and talk."

As Erin wondered about his frown, hot sparks shot up her arm at his firm, warm handshake. She extracted her hand and words stuck in her throat like a glob of peanut butter. She had finally fulfilled her mother's dream. She was speechless.

Jared pulled his brows together tighter. "Is that all right?"

Erin cleared her throat, thrown off balance by the ribbons of fire shooting from her hand into her bloodstream and by how unhappy he looked to be meeting her. It didn't bode well for the interview. "Uh, sure, sure, whatever you say," she said, hoping the warm blush she felt spreading through her face wasn't too obvious. "I'll wait over there for you." She gestured to a blue flowered couch against the far wall.

He nodded and Erin walked over to the overstuffed couch and sat down. She took a deep breath and plastered a calm expression on her face. Heavens, she hoped her strange reaction to him was only surprise at finding him to be so good-looking yet so unflashy—at least on the outside. Whatever the case, with her house on the line, this was the wrong time to get in a muddle over a man.

But as she sat and waited, her eyes kept wandering in Jared's direction to watch his capable movements behind the counter. She couldn't help but notice how his muscled torso bunched and moved beneath his blue shirt as he reached for coffee mugs and made cappuccino.

When he came out from behind the counter and headed her way, she bit her lip hard. Figured. His bottom half was just as well put together as his top half. When he turned and greeted a customer, she found her interested gaze glued to his backside.

"Wow," she whispered, her jaw hanging. He had the cutest, tightest pair of buns she'd ever seen.

She dragged her gaze away and closed her mouth, wondering why she was so enthralled by Jared Warfield. Maybe she'd been alone for too long. Yes, that was it. Not allowing a man in her life since Brent, who had cut out her heart, was obviously the problem. She was sure any reasonably attractive guy would have the same effect on her.

Relaxing, she leaned over and rummaged in her briefcase for her small tape recorder. She reminded herself it really didn't matter how movie-star gorgeous this Warfield guy was. She didn't need or want a man now, especially not after her disastrous marriage and gut-wrenching divorce.

As if the only man, other than her father, that she'd ever loved walking out on her wasn't bad enough, the icing on the cake had been when Brent had announced he was broke because of bad investments. The day their divorce had been final, she'd sewn her tattered heart back together as best she could, thrown out all of Brent's stuff, sworn off men and promised herself to avoid anything resembling love. She intended to stick to that vow and concentrate on writing her story, digging herself out of debt and saving her house and her self-respect. No man was worth the heartache or distraction, not even one with café au lait eyes and a body to die for.

Though he would rather shove bamboo under his fingernails than give an interview, Jared moved toward the stunning redhead from the *Beacon,* still puzzled by her strange behavior. A few minutes ago she'd looked downright flustered. He shrugged irritably and passed it off as simple embarrassment for mistaking Dan for himself.

Of course, she could just be putting her antennae up to scope him out, like he'd seen loads of women do to the Warfield men, hoping to marry a millionaire.

Balancing a mocha cappuccino in one hand and a plate laden with a fresh apple turnover in the other, he navigated over to the reporter. Hopefully this interview would be done soon and he could get back to work. He resented wasting his time on this stuff. He'd only consented because Warfield's needed the publicity. If not for Warfield's, he wouldn't go anywhere near the press. He had Allison to think of now.

When he arrived at the couch, the reporter looked up at him, her beautiful moss-green eyes glinting behind her tortoiseshell glasses.

"Thanks for waiting." He set the cappuccino and pastry down on the low coffee table in front of the couch, ignoring his sudden, strange urge to study those eyes and her flawless, creamy skin. Lowering himself into the wing chair behind him, he told himself to loosen up. He'd give a few stock answers and then send the reporter on her way. "Okay. Let's get started."

"Do you make a habit of working behind the counter?" she asked, her brows raised.

He sensed the surprise behind her question. "Not usually, but we're short on help today, and I pitch in where I'm needed. I started Warfield's with one store and one employee, so I've had plenty of experience waiting on customers."

She picked up a small tape recorder. "Do you mind if I tape this interview?"

His first instinct was to refuse; why make her job easier? But it wasn't as if he had anything against this particular reporter. Besides, he reminded himself, Warfield's would benefit from a spread in the *Beacon*. "No, not at all," he replied, striving to keep the impatience from his voice. "And help yourself to the cappuccino and apple turnover."

She pulled her mouth into a tiny smile. "I love apple turnovers and cappuccino." She picked the flaky pastry up and took a big bite. "Thank you," she mumbled.

He smiled. Her enjoyment of the pastry, one of his own favorites, pleased him. Maybe this interview wouldn't be so bad after all. Relaxing against the back of the chair, he drew his leg up and propped his ankle on the opposite knee, liking the sight of her unselfconsciously demolishing the turnover.

He knew he shouldn't stare but did, anyway, letting his gaze wander over her rose-tinted face, liking the light freckles that dusted her straight, just-the-right-size nose. He wondered if that thick mane of auburn curls falling like waves of flame to below her shoulders was as soft as it looked. He wished he could run his fingers through the fiery strands to find out.

Enjoying his exploration, he let his eyes roam lower, taking in her full lips, the exact color of the delicate carnations he'd planted in his backyard. Drawing a deep breath, he moved his gaze downward past her blue skirt to her legs. Though her skirt wasn't particularly short, it still displayed her legs below her knees. And what perfect, stunning legs they were, willowy and curved exactly the way he liked.

His heart began to beat heavily in his chest. Heat enveloped him. He looked back up and found her delicately licking pastry sugar from her fingers. He stifled a groan, unable to help watching in blatant fascination as her pink tongue came out and cleaned her fingers of sugar, one…by one…by one. Swallowing, he averted his gaze again, fighting for control, and repositioned his watch on his wrist.

Don't go there, buddy. Don't want what you don't need. Getting hung up on a reporter would be the one, surefire way to expose little Allison to the rabid media, which had burned him before.

When he looked back at Ms. James, she had thankfully finished cleaning her fingers. She flicked on the tape recorder. "First, I'm going to ask you some questions, like your age and what you like to do. Then I'll let you talk for a while, all right?"

He nodded tersely.

She scooched over on the couch until she sat just a foot from him. Her delicate scent—roses—floated over him, and he fought the urge to sniff the air and drag in more of the wonderful, feminine smell through his nose. The last time he'd smelled anything that good was while standing in the middle of his flower beds when they were in full bloom.

"How old are you?" she asked.

"Thirty-two." He tried to make his voice sound like her perfume wasn't wreaking havoc with his senses.

"And have you always lived in Portland?"

"Uh-huh."

"Soooo…what are your interests?" She licked at the sugary coating on her lips again.

He watched her tongue stroke her lip, and the heat in his body was stoked back to life. "Uh, interests?"

She pursed her sugary lips, then picked up her cappuccino. "You know, hobbies, likes, dislikes. That kind of thing."

Jared ruthlessly forced his eyes, and thoughts, away from her mouth and how much he wanted to take care of that sugar himself. "Well, I like to ski and work in my garden—"

She stopped midsip and looked at him over the rim of the cup. "You like to garden?"

He lifted a brow and nodded. "Sure. I grow enough vegetables to keep me supplied all summer."

"Oh, come on." She put her cup down. "You grow your own vegetables?"

He gave her a stony glare, feeling his strange attraction being replaced by his earlier irritation and wariness. "Yes, I do, Ms. James. I also like to cook. Surprised?"

"Quite frankly, I am," she said, tucking some stray

strands of hair behind her ear. "Most men like you wouldn't want to get their hands messy enough to garden or cook. I figured you'd be more interested in fast cars, wild parties and loose women in lingerie, stuff like that."

He clenched his jaw and dropped his foot to the floor. Loose women in lingerie? Damn, how he hated what everyone expected him to be, the wealthy guy without a care in the world, tooling around in his hot car, chasing women day and night. Sure, he had nice things and a nice car, but he'd worked his butt off to make Warfield's what it was today and to enjoy the perks that came with being a successful business owner. And, yeah, he'd had his share of chasing women in his younger days, but he was over that now that he had Allison in his life.

"I guess I'm not like most men, then, am I?" he said, just managing to be civil.

Her gaze flicked down and held on his wristwatch for a long, significant moment. "Well, most men don't have trust funds to live on, do they?" Her mouth spread into a tight, judgmental smile.

He clenched his hands. His instincts about this interview had proved dead-on. The press was bad news. They'd ridden his back his whole life, always groveling for some kind of story about his famous family. And then, before he'd threatened one reporter with libel a year ago, they'd tried to do a hatchet job when his half sister, Carolyn, had died.

The media had been too damn eager to exploit the circumstances of the famous Janet Worthington's daughter's death. Not only had a slew of reporters hounded him for details of the motorcycle crash that had snuffed out Carolyn's life, they'd jumped on him like a pack of wolves when he'd adopted Carolyn's six-month-old baby daughter, Allison. The press had wanted to splash her picture across the front page. Man, how Carolyn would have hated that.

The familiar guilt for failing to save Carolyn jabbed at him, fueling his desire to cut this interview short. He knew he was overreacting, but this snooty reporter had managed to push his buttons, right off the bat. Ms. James might be really nice to look at but she was obviously nothing but a self-serving reporter out to dig up dirt.

He rose, staring her down. "Trust funds? How do you know what the hell I live on?"

She blinked and pushed her glasses up her nose. "Uh, well…" She hesitated, clearly unprepared for his sudden turnabout. Luckily he had been prepared for *her* ambush.

Jared didn't wait for her to say more. "Your interview's over, sweetheart." He leaned down and deliberately placed his hands on the coffee table and bent in close. Her scent washed over him again, but his anger doused its effect. "For your information, I've worked damned hard to get to where I am today and I don't need you turning your pert little nose up at my lifestyle." He straightened and sent her a hard glare. "Go find someone else to insult." He turned to walk away.

"Mr. Warfield?"

Something in her soft tone made him stop, his hands still fisted at his sides. He didn't turn around.

"I chose you for this article because you have the kind of lifestyle our readers want to read about. Unfortunately, I guess, money is part of your life. It's my job to write the story my editor wants."

Unmoved, he swiveled back to face her. She might not have been technically out of line, but she'd implied that he was a lazy idiot who had nothing better to do than piddle away his inheritance. She'd struck right at the heart of one of his biggest pet peeves: people who assumed he'd ridden his father's coattails to instant wealth. Her rude assumptions were so far from the truth that they would be laughable if they didn't make him so angry. He hadn't used one penny of the Warfield millions to build his business, which he was damn proud of.

Yeah, he would follow his instincts on this one. To hell with her story. He was out of here.

"Too bad." He ignored how her pretty green eyes widened in stunned surprise. "You can go back to your editor and tell him this rich guy changed his mind. The interview's off."

He stalked off and left her sitting on the couch with her sugary mouth hanging open and her tape recorder still running.

Heart pounding, Erin watched Jared walk away toward a door at the back of the store, unable to resist taking one last peek at the rear view of his perfect male body. The guy had just told her to take a hike, yet she could still feel the pulse of her attraction sizzling through her body like an electric current. Who would have guessed a man could turn her on while telling her off?

But that didn't matter. Her desperation was what counted here. What had possessed her to bring up loose women in lingerie? She'd blown it, big-time.

Nibbling a nail, Erin acknowledged she'd been thrown off whack ever since she saw Jared standing behind the counter. Had her neglected libido sent her good judgment flying out the window? That had to be the problem. What else could have caused her to alienate part of her biggest story opportunity in months, jeopardizing her only chance to pay off Brent's debts and save her house in one fell swoop?

Shaking her head, she flicked her tape recorder off,

fighting away panic. What now? She sat and munched on her turnover, but the sweet sugar and tart apples suddenly tasted like sawdust.

She had to admit, Jared wasn't what she'd expected. She'd been ready for a shallow jerk. Instead she'd met with a gorgeous male with fathomless brown eyes, a body like a Greek god and an interest in growing vegetables, for goodness sakes! If he'd told her he was a leprechaun from Ireland she wouldn't have been more surprised. He had to be putting on an act for the interview. She'd noticed his Rolex watch and designer label khakis. He might *look* normal from a distance, but he probably wasn't. Brent had worn the same designer pants and had sported a similar watch.

Despite glimpses of tantalizing ordinariness, Jared was more than likely a replica of Brent, which would be too bad if she were in the market for a man. She definitely wasn't, though she could easily lose herself in Jared's sexy eyes and intensely appreciate his big, male body. She might have sworn off men, but apparently she wasn't dead.

Reality check. Even though Jared Warfield had brought her stupid body back to life, Brent's success at ripping her heart out made Jared off-limits. But for an instant, that cute, normal, cashier guy had been her fantasy man come true.

She snorted under her breath. So much for fantasies. After Brent she knew better than to believe in dreams. How could she forget the scorn he'd hurled at her until there was nothing left but the bitter knowledge that she was just as useless to Brent as she had been to her mother?

Brent had hammered that message into her heart with a nail when he'd left her.

Standing, she fingered the chain around her neck, the one tangible thing she had to remind herself how important it was not to love any man again. She fought off her bad memories and the gathering sense of doom, then picked up her stuff, took one long swig of her cappuccino and headed out the door. Warm air surrounded her, and she raised her face to the sun, trying to let the gorgeous September day ease the frustration of ruining her interview.

She made a left on the sidewalk and walked back toward her office. She came to the end of the block and waited for the signal to change, searching her mind for a rich bachelor she might have missed in her search for interview subjects. But she came up empty. Jared was her last hope. She *had* to get that bonus.

Suddenly a familiar tune caught her ear. She turned toward the sound and realized the music came from a late model, bright-red BMW convertible sedan with its top down in the street in front of her. She glanced at the driver. And blinked. Jared. The expensive sports car wasn't a surprise. What *was* a shocker was that he was singing along with the seventies tune on the radio while a huge, shaggy dog buckled in the front passenger seat of the car, his furry head thrown back, howled along with him.

The two of them were singing their hearts out, in perfect unison. Though horribly off-key, as she would expect, the dog could sing. She chuckled under her breath. She'd never seen or heard anything like it before.

The light and the walk signal changed. As Jared pulled away, Erin noticed a child's car seat in the back next to a dog crate much too small for the dog in the front seat. She also caught a glimpse of the car's license plate, which simply read Coffee.

Surprise froze her to the curb. Gardening. A howling dog. A kid's car seat? Jared Warfield was becoming more of a mystery by the minute. Since she'd been pressed for time, she had done only minimal research on Jared, but she was certain she hadn't read anything about a child. As far as she knew, he'd never even been married. She found herself intrigued. Was he hiding a love child? Or was he secretly married? It would be interesting to peel back the layers to the real man beneath—along with his clothes, of course.

Sirens went off in her brain. What was she thinking? A droolworthy, loaded guy was the last person she should spend any time with. But she had to see him again whether she liked it or not. She needed that bonus desperately, and her reporter's instincts told her she wouldn't get it without Jared featured in her article. He was a hot commodity right now, and his family was famous in Portland. If she didn't interview him, somebody else would and she'd lose out. No, she couldn't give up on interviewing "Hunk" Warfield.

Then again, "Elvis" Warfield seemed appropriate. When she thought about it, so did "Farmer" Warfield. And "Daddy" Warfield, too. As she started walking again, she wondered if Jared was really what he seemed—an ordinary man who liked dogs and kids and who would undoubtedly love a woman the way she'd always dreamed of, with his heart and soul and everything in him?

A man so different from Brent.

No. That man didn't exist. Even so, her insides melted at the thought of someone loving her, reminding her of how long it had been since anyone had really cared about her, how many years had passed since her father had died while illegally racing his souped-up '67 Mustang.

She reached up again and grasped the dime-store chain that had once held the sapphire ring he'd given her a few days before he'd died. Oh, how she wished he'd loved her enough not to risk his life racing cars. Unfortunately, the ring was gone now....

Erin closed her eyes for a moment, reliving the pain of the day her mom had yanked the chain from around Erin's neck to pawn the ring for cash. Fighting off a wave of grief and yearning, she forced herself to focus on her predicament rather than her innumerable old hurts. She was totally intrigued with a man who would probably stick pins in a voodoo doll with red hair, given the chance.

How was she going to dig herself out of this mess? She didn't have a clue, but she wasn't about to roll over and let fate knock her to her knees again. Not after the sheer hell Brent had put her through. One way or another she'd get her interview and the bonus, and she'd satisfy her reporter's curiosity and discover exactly what kind of man Jared was—without drooling.

She turned the corner, again noticing the beautiful day, complete with clear blue sky, warm, calming breeze and green trees gently rustling in the light wind. It was too lovely a day for her life to fall apart. Yes, she would turn Jared around. She had to.

Failure simply wasn't an option.

Chapter Two

Erin stepped through the door leading to the roof of Jared's office building and shielded her eyes from the bright sun and intense blue sky. She hung back, gathering her courage, mentally rehearsing what she was going to say to him.

When she'd returned to her office yesterday after she'd seen Jared and the singing dog, she'd done a little research on Mr. Warfield. She'd found oodles of information about his father, who was a business icon in Portland, having made a fortune in commercial real estate investments.

She'd come across a little information about his half sister, who'd had problems with drugs and was the daughter of Janet Worthington, a former Hollywood actress who'd died of cancer three years ago. She'd also found a bit of information on Jared, mostly stories about Warfield's, especially in its early days when coffeehouses were still novel. But she'd hit the jackpot when she'd found an article in another paper about Jared adopting his niece when his sister died in a motorcycle crash.

Bingo. The mysterious car seat had been explained. Jared was a dad to his adopted niece.

Even though she had her answer about the car seat, she still needed to convince Jared to give her an interview. Taking a deep breath, she pressed a shaking hand to her twisting, rolling stomach, her white silk blouse sticking to her damp palm, praying that the sparks and heat she'd felt at Warfield's were nothing but a fluke.

She glanced around, taking in the colorful rooftop garden Jared had presumably created, and suppressed an inward cringe. He *did* like to garden. Way to go, Erin.

She spotted Jared in the corner, squatting with his wide back turned, his hands buried in a large pot. Her stomach somersaulted again, and her heart jumped in her chest like a hyper kangaroo. With a muttered oath, she backed up a few steps, urging herself to calm down.

After she'd sucked in several long breaths and dried her hand on her beige linen skirt, she moved forward again, summoning up the courage to speak. "Mr....Mr. Warfield?" Oh, great start. She sounded like a scared little girl about to confront the boogeyman.

He snapped his head around, his face pressed into a surprised frown, then stood. Walking toward her, a crease in his brow, he wiped his hands on the denim work apron he wore over a pale-yellow oxford shirt that made his eyes look like dark, creamy chocolate. "How did *you* get here?"

Erin raised her chin, trying to ignore how he loomed over her, the masculine breadth of his shoulders blocking the bright sun and azure sky from her view. "Your secretary told me where you were."

"Really? Now why would she do that when I gave very specific instructions not to be disturbed?"

Erin uneasily lifted a shoulder, forcing herself to display

a nonchalance she hadn't felt since she'd laid eyes on Jared yesterday. "I sort of told her I had a few more questions to ask you."

"A few more? Did you forget to mention that I canceled the interview?"

She glanced down, wishing she were a better liar. "I, uh, might have forgotten to mention that, yes."

"What do you want?"

She suppressed a flinch at his rude tone, smiled tremulously and stood her ground, forcing herself to remember what was at stake despite the anxiety ripping her insides apart like razors. "I came to apologize for my... unprofessional behavior."

He narrowed his eyes. "And what else?" He crossed his arms over his broad chest. "You didn't come here just to apologize."

He was right, and it was time to quit quaking in her boots, get the job done and claw her way out of the hole she'd dug for herself.

She swallowed. "Actually, Mr. Warfield, I was hoping you'd reconsider and consent to the interview—"

"Why should I?"

"Because you promised you'd give it?" she asked, hoping to appeal to his sense of fair play—if he had one.

He shook his head. "I never agreed to be insulted and pigeonholed with all of the other jerky men in the world."

She held up her hands. "I know, but I think we got off on the wrong foot. I'm much too outspoken, it's my biggest fault. I'd like to start over."

He squatted down and put his hands in another pot. "I'm sure you would, but that's impossible. I only agreed to the interview because my advertising people thought it would be good publicity. But no publicity is worth being badgered about my money or lifestyle."

While she didn't really think she'd badgered him exactly, she would say anything to convince him to give her a second chance. "Can I explain?"

Without waiting for him to reply she kept going. "I...I'd had several other interviews and all of them were the epitome of the spoiled, lazy rich guy. I guess I assumed you were, too. I made a mistake and I'm very sorry I offended you." She paused and drew a deep breath, prepared to beg. "I really need this story. Please, won't you reconsider? I know the story idea is a little lame and the date you'd have to go on might be awkward—"

He swung his head around. "Date? What date?"

"That's part of the article. The *Beacon* features you in the Saturday edition, and then women write in and try to convince you to take them on a date. My editor chooses a winner and then—"

"No way." He rose and rubbed the dirt from his hands. "No one but me chooses who I date. Sorry, Ms. James, my decision stands." He untied his apron, yanked it off and threw it in a box of gardening supplies next to the door. "If you'll excuse me?"

As she vaguely wondered why Jared seemed so against one little date, panic seeped through her. With as much bravado as she could muster, she shoved the desperate feeling aside. This wasn't the time to become spineless.

Jared stepped past her and moved to the stairwell. She followed him, noticing how nicely his well-muscled shoulders flowed into his narrow waist and tight rear end. She jerked her thoughts away from his body, back to the pressing problem at hand. "Please, Mr. Warfield. I need this interview, and the publicity *would* be good for business."

"I don't need the publicity that bad," he said, stomping down the stairs.

"But you just said your marketing department thought

it was a good idea,'' she said, struggling to keep up with his hasty descent down the stairwell. "Think of it as free advertising.''

He held up his hands, then turned and unlocked the door to his office. "Look, Ms. James, I appreciate your effort.'' He pushed the door open. "But I've made my decision—''

A tiny, white puppy exploded from the small office and jumped at Jared's legs.

All thoughts of the article disappeared from Erin's head. "Oh, look at that! What a sweetheart.'' She squatted and held her arms out. "Come over here, puppy.''

The fluffy puppy bounded over to Erin and launched itself into her arms. Enchanted, Erin flopped sideways onto the carpeted floor as best she could in her skirt and held the dog close, taking every single kiss the enthusiastic puppy had to dole out.

She loved dogs. She'd had a dog once, a fluffy mutt her dad had named Max. But her dad died when she was eight, and so her mom had given the dog away, claiming Max made her allergies flare up. Erin had never been aware of any allergies and said so, but it hadn't made any difference. The dog was gone within hours, to where, Erin never knew. She'd cried for days, in private, of course. Her mom found fault with almost everything Erin did, but displays of emotion topped the list.

"What a cutie-pie you are, yes you are.'' She stroked the puppy's curly fur and planted kisses on its fuzzy head, falling headfirst into memories of her dad and Max. The three of them had spent hours together on walks and playing at the park. Those days, spent with her dad, were the only time in her life she'd felt truly loved and cared for. Of course, true to the pattern in her life since, her happiness had come to an abrupt end when he'd died.

After a few melancholy moments she pulled herself out

of her reverie, sensing the force of Jared's burnished gaze. She glanced up at him, noting his puckered brow. Uneasiness slid through her.

He cocked a slight smile. "Do you really love dogs, or are you just trying to soften me up to get your interview?"

She clambered to her feet, the puppy still in her arms, and smoothed her skirt down at the hips. She gazed at him frankly. "Look, I love dogs with or without the interview." She shook her head, perplexed. "What could my love of animals possibly have to do with the interview, anyway?"

"You could pretend to like dogs so I'd look down and think how cute you two look together and—"

She handed the pup back to him. "Yes, well, that's a little farfetched. I reacted the way I always do when I see a cute baby animal. I got down on the floor to play." Erin's curiosity about what drove Jared, already piqued, rose even higher. Why was he so wary about every little thing she said and did?

She looked directly in his eyes and raised an inquisitive brow. "You don't trust me very much, do you, Mr. Warfield?"

"I don't particularly distrust you, Ms. James," he said slowly, obviously choosing his words carefully. "I'm sorry if I offended you, but I've learned to be cautious around the press."

She would love to know why he was so skittish. Fortunately, she wouldn't know him long enough to find out, and she doubted her article would delve that deep. And this certainly didn't seem like the time to press him about his daughter. "I've noticed that."

She leaned toward him and nuzzled the pup in his arms. Realizing how close she was, she stiffened and looked up. Her eyes met his and their gazes held. Silence strung out between them, taut and tense. She was so close she could smell his scent, coffee and earth, swirling around her. Sparks of awareness tingled along her skin. Her heart leaped. Obviously, the attraction she'd felt earlier was not a one-time thing.

His gaze flicked to her lips and stopped, and her body tightened. She swayed toward him, wishing with everything in her that he would close the distance between them and press that wicked mouth against hers for a long, deep kiss.

The puppy yipped, breaking the spell, scrambling Erin's control like eggs in a sizzling frying pan. She took a quick step back and drew in a ragged breath. Man, Jared was hot. His smell and gorgeous body were enough to make *control* a foreign word.

Enough, already! Shocked, Erin moved back another step and ripped her gaze from his, hoping he didn't notice her blush. She scrabbled for control, focusing her wayward attention on what she'd come here for. Her story. The bonus. Financial salvation.

"So, about the interview?" she asked, proud of how normal she'd made her voice sound after she'd almost burst into flames.

He turned and moved behind his neat-as-a pin, heavy wood desk, an expression on his face she couldn't decipher. "Still after that story."

She regarded him solemnly. "It's my job."

He tucked the puppy under one arm and looked through some papers on his desk with his free hand, but didn't speak right away. Her heart pounding, Erin waited for an answer.

Finally he looked up, his face hard. "I'm sorry, Ms. James."

Erin fought the panic spreading through her, grasping at

straws in a last-ditch effort to change his mind. "Even if I let you have final approval of the article?"

He hesitated, then shook his head. "No."

The burn of defeat spread through her, creating a lump in her throat the size of a boulder. She vaguely wondered how she was going to clean up the gigantic financial mess Brent had saddled her with and how she was going to complete "The Bachelor Chronicles."

She nodded woodenly and pressed her lips together to keep them from trembling. "I guess...I guess I'll go now," she managed to say. She wished she could forget this story and Jared Warfield and everything else that had happened in the past two days.

And then, because she had no choice, she turned and walked away, hoping she would wake up and discover this was all just a bad dream.

Jared watched Erin leave, admiring her slender legs from the back, loving the way her curvy hips moved under her skirt.

When she was gone, he rubbed Josie behind her ears and tried to regain control of his body, floored at how close he'd come to kissing Erin a few minutes earlier. Thank goodness Josie had let out that bark in the nick of time.

Despite his irritation over the pull he felt toward Erin, he still wondered if he shouldn't have given her the damn interview. If marketing said Warfield's needed the publicity, then Warfield's needed the publicity.

Oh, man. Had he let his desire to protect Allison intrude on his good business sense? Maybe he should call Erin back.

The sizzling look they'd shared was incentive enough, as was the way she'd looked sitting on the floor with Josie, her skirt hiked up above her knees, her long, shapely legs exposed. With her auburn curls framing her face and her moss-colored eyes sparkling with delight, she'd looked like a woodland goddess come to life.

He brought his thoughts up short. He met beautiful women every day. Why was he even thinking about calling back this woman reporter? Why should he trust the media, especially now, when he and Allison were finally taking baby steps toward recovering from the heart-tearing grief of Carolyn's death?

No. The last thing he needed was to get tangled up with Erin James, or any other woman for that matter. All of his father's wives had left him, and he'd died alone and miserable, and that had taught Jared an important lesson: never let a woman worm her way into his life only to leave him or take advantage of him in the end. He had to protect himself, and now he had Allison to think about, too.

No way was he going to mess up his precious daughter's life by getting involved with a woman. Sure, he dated occasionally to satisfy his need for social activity, among other things. But drinks and dinner, usually never with the same woman more than a few times, were as far as his dating ever went. He made it a point not to date anyone he might be tempted to bring home, or anyone who might want to get her hooks into a millionaire—and that seemed to be everybody. He avoided emotional entanglements like a dreaded disease.

And Erin was a reporter, to boot. No way was he going to let some gossip-chasing journalist close enough to hurt Allison.

No. Erin James was out for her story and would probably exploit him given the chance. Flower-colored lips and leaf-speckled eyes couldn't change that. Nothing could. Resolutely he vowed to put the whole thing from his mind.

He'd never wanted to do the interview, and now he wouldn't have to.

He put Josie in her crate next to his desk, then leaned back in his chair, fiddling with his watch, waiting for relief to surface.

A few minutes later his eighteen-month-old daughter, Allison, appeared in the doorway holding her nanny, Mrs. Sloane's, hand. "Hi, Dada!" Allison crowed, waving. She ran into his office and jumped into his outstretched arms, looking absolutely adorable in light-blue pants and a pink top with fuzzy yellow bunnies all over it.

He pulled her close and buried his head in her wispy, blond curls, loving how her baby-fresh hair tickled his nose. "Ally-Bear. What a nice surprise." He gave Mrs. Sloane a questioning look.

She smoothed her gray hair, pulled back in its customary bun, and smiled indulgently at Allison, her gray eyes sparkling. "She wanted to come visit her daddy. I hope you don't mind."

"Of course not." He pressed his mouth to Allison's neck and made raspberry sounds. "I'm always happy to see my pretty girl."

Allison chortled in delight and squirmed away. "Tickly, Dada." She pulled back and plopped down on his lap, then maneuvered herself around and scooted out until she sat just behind his knees. "Horsey, Dada, horsey!"

Smiling, Jared put his hands under her arms and moved his legs up and down in a jerky, horselike fashion. "We're going on a ride, Ally-Bear. Hold on!" he playfully warned, then moved his legs faster and faster.

Allison shrieked in delight.

Jared had never heard a more wonderful, happy sound in his life. He didn't want to do anything that might threaten his angel, something that might someday give her a reason not to giggle her heart out.

He made the choice then and there not to second-guess his decision to back out of the interview. Erin James had gotten his back up from the get-go. He didn't trust her, and he never would. Too much was at stake to risk opening up to her. He'd forget everything remotely connected with the delectable reporter and put his darling Allison first.

Allison laughed again, and the sound echoed within his heart, filling a space that he'd always thought would be empty. Allison was all he needed.

Case closed. He'd do everything possible to stay away from Erin James, no matter how good she smelled.

Erin looked up from the legal pad on her lap. "Come on," she said to her best friend, Colleen. "Get over here and help me. I need to figure out how to get this interview."

Colleen glared at her over the door of Erin's refrigerator and shoved her blond curls out of her eyes. "Would you cool your jets? You burned dinner, so I'm starving."

Erin pressed her lips together and pushed up her glasses. Colleen was no help at all. "How can you think about food at a time like this? My future's at stake here."

The fridge door slammed. Colleen stalked into the living room, an apple in her hand. "And whose fault is that, I wonder?" she said, her eyebrows lifted high, a mock-accusatory look on her face.

Erin raised her hands in surrender. "I know, I know, I blew it. You don't have to say it again."

"Oh, but I do," Colleen said, her mouth curved into a satisfied smile. "For the first time in ages a man's gotten to you. This day has been long in coming."

Erin dropped her shoulders and gave her friend a dispassionate look. "Would you get serious? He hasn't 'gotten to me' at all."

"You get serious. You haven't been with a man in more than two years. It was only a matter of time before your self-imposed celibacy landed you in trouble."

"It wasn't that at all," Erin said, only half believing the statement herself. "It was my big mouth, as usual." And her darn curiosity.

"Maybe so, but you said yourself this guy was good-looking. Would you have blown the interview if he looked like Elmer Fudd?"

Erin hesitated. Colleen had made a good point. The disgusting truth was, Erin had been nothing but a big old mass of need since she'd clung to Jared's hot, interested gaze over the puppy's head. It looked like her plan to avoid being affected by men had backfired.

"Okay, Miss Smarty-Pants, you're right," Erin finally said. "I'm attracted to him. But that's pointless, and so is analyzing why I messed up the interview." She gazed speculatively at Colleen. "Did I tell you I discovered Jared adopted his niece when his sister died a year ago?"

"Yes, I think you've mentioned it a time or two," Colleen mumbled around a chunk of apple.

Erin lifted one shoulder. "Okay, I'll admit that bit of information intrigues me. I mean, how many single guys would adopt a child?"

"Not many," Colleen admitted. "Pretty fascinated by this guy, aren't you? Do I sense a romance in the making?"

Erin stared at Colleen, her friend's question restoring Erin's vow not to be so darn interested in Jared, aside from the interview she needed. "No, you don't. I'm not fascinated. All I'm interested in is finding a way to get the job done, not encourage a romance."

"Okay. So what about sex?"

Erin wasn't at all surprised by Colleen's statement. With Colleen, everything came down to sex. Erin looked at her as if she was a dull child. "This isn't about sex. It's about getting that bonus."

Colleen slid her gaze to Erin, her blue eyes gleaming. "Of course it's about sex. Men relate to sex better than anything. Use it to get the interview."

Erin blinked and widened her eyes. "You think I should...have sex with him to get the interview?"

"Of course not! Just use your sexuality to soften him up. More than one man has been known to give in to a sexy, confident woman."

Colleen's idea sounded stupid. Erin was hardly sexy, and she was feeling far from confident about this situation. Yet, Jared *had* stared back today. Though she'd been out of commission for a while, Erin knew the look of an appreciative male when she saw it. But using that to her advantage seemed...well, sleazy. Though she'd used some sly tactics in the past to get a story, she'd never used sex to do her job. Besides, she thought, glancing down at her baggy sweats and toe socks, she would never be enough of a femme fatale to pull it off.

She bit her lip, remembering how Brent had called her a fat cow the day he'd left her. The wound on her heart throbbed.

Self-consciously pulling her sweatshirt down over her hips, she shook her head. "No way," she stated emphatically. "Sex is out of the question."

Colleen snorted. "I wasn't suggesting you strip naked and jump on him. Use what you've got to soften him up."

Erin let out a laugh and gestured to herself with a flick of her hand. "This is all I've got."

"Give yourself some credit. You have great legs, fantastic hair and gorgeous eyes. Use those things to capture and hold Warfield's interest to get the interview.''

Erin pulled her pencil from behind her ear and chewed on it. Maybe Colleen was right. It wouldn't have to go far; just a little apologizing, flirting, maybe a flash of leg...

The thought of dealing with Jared under those circumstances sent a major swarm of butterflies into her stomach. Lord, she didn't know if she could face him again. But she was desperate, and she hadn't come up with any other bright ideas. She had one more shot to get the interview and the bonus. Drastic measures seemed appropriate.

She looked at her friend's stylish blond hairstyle and flattering outfit. ''Would you help me do this?'' she asked, feeling a sense of insecurity.

Colleen wagged her eyebrows. ''You want me to come along and coach from the sidelines?''

''Of course not.'' The last thing she needed was an audience to witness her trying to attract a man. ''But I could use some advice on clothes and makeup. What do you think?''

Colleen smiled conspiratorially and rubbed her hands together. ''You've come to the right place. Let's get to work.''

Erin did her best to return Colleen's smile, but found it difficult. She was an absolute lunatic for thinking she could attract a man like Jared Warfield, even as part of a weird plot to convince him to give her the interview.

Brent's merciless treatment had struck an almost fatal blow to her self-confidence.

But she had to stuff her doubts, forget about the damage Brent had caused and take the chance. She might lose her dignity, but thank goodness she didn't have to worry about losing her heart.

* * *

Jared read the card he'd found attached to the small, flat gift, wrapped in flowery tissue paper and curly ribbon.

Dear Mr. Warfield:
Please accept this gift as a token of my regret regarding our conversation yesterday. I am officially ready to eat crow and conduct a proper interview. I would love to have you as my guest for lunch today at The Viceroy at noon. See you then.

Sincerely, Erin James.

He shook his head and reached for the heavy package and quickly tore the flimsy tissue aside. Inside was a beautifully done book on flowers of the Pacific Northwest. A smile curved his lips at the significance of the subject matter; Ms. James was trying to make up for her inappropriate comments about his love for gardening.

While he admired her persistence, he still had no intention of granting her the interview and going on some ridiculous, arranged date. Glancing at the picture of Allison on his desk, her four new teeth visible behind her cute little smile, he reminded himself of his vow to keep the media out of their lives for good.

But he might meet Erin for lunch just to see the look on her face when he showed up and refused to talk about himself. This had become a challenge, something he often couldn't resist. Yes, that was it, this was a game, nothing more. Accepting her invitation had nothing to do with her sexy green eyes, curvy legs and tousled hair that he would love to touch. Nope. Nothing at all.

A light knock on his door pulled his attention away from Erin James and her damn interview.

"Come in," he said.

Mark Phillips, Warfield's head of marketing, stepped

through the partially open door, his dark eyebrows knitted together. "You got a minute?"

Jared nodded and waved him in. "Sure."

Mark, whose small stature made him look all of twenty instead of his actual age of thirty-three, stepped in the room and held up a file folder. "The quarterly sales figures," he said grimly.

Jared raised his eyebrows. "Not good?"

Mark lowered himself into the chair opposite Jared's desk and rubbed his chin, his brown eyes reflecting concern. "Not terrible, but not great. As expected, we've slipped a notch or two."

Jared reached for the folder. "Anything serious?"

"Maybe."

That single word sent concern skipping through Jared like a flat rock on water. Frowning, Jared picked up the file and flipped it open. A few minutes later he'd finished scanning the figures. Mark was right. Sales had fallen off over the past six months.

He turned to Mark. "What's causing this?"

Mark shrugged his suit-jacketed shoulders. Despite Warfield's casual-dress policy, he still wore a suit to work every day. "It's hard to say. Could just be the natural business cycle. But my gut feeling is it's the competition, which is keen right now. Luckily that bachelor article will be out soon. A free bit of publicity could help."

Shifting uneasily, Jared picked up a paper clip and bent it out of shape. A sharp needle of guilt joined the concern roiling in his gut. "I canceled the interview."

Mark laughed under his breath. "You're kidding, right?" He jerked his tie loose and unbuttoned the top button on his dress shirt.

"Nope. The reporter they sent was rude." Eye candy, but still rude.

"So you backed out?"

He glared at Mark and mentally dug in his heels, remembering Allison. "Yeah, I backed out. I never wanted to do the interview to begin with, and they wanted me to go on some date."

Mark leaned forward. "Jared, we need this publicity. I think you should reconsider the interview."

Jared scowled and twisted the paper clip. "We've been over this, Mark. I don't think the interview is necessary."

"Even after you've seen those sales figures?"

Jared hesitated and clenched his jaw tight, hating being pressured to do something that could blow up in his face. "The timing's bad," he muttered, looking for an excuse to back out.

"Nothing has changed. Publicity is publicity, any way you look at it, even if it involves a perfunctory date." Mark leaned back in his chair. "We can't afford to pass this up. What if they go for Ryan Cavanaugh? Then Java Joint gets the exposure. Is that what you want?"

Jared considered Mark's words. Cavanaugh was a bachelor and very eligible. And he'd probably love to get the jump on Warfield's and snag the interview and publicity. Could Jared afford to take that chance? Though he hated to admit it, the decision had been taken out of his hands. He'd have to be sure to leave Allison out of the interview and hope Ms. James hadn't dug deep enough to discover he'd adopted his niece. He would worry about the date later. He'd definitely find a way to get out of that part of the agreement.

"All right," he conceded. "I'll do the interview. But I don't like this one bit."

Mark smiled and rose. "How bad can it be? Just give the reporter a few tidbits, show up for the date, and that will be it."

He raised a brow as Mark left, then roughly adjusted his watch on his wrist. Tidbits? Somehow he doubted Erin James would be satisfied with mere tidbits. She seemed pretty desperate to get the interview, probably because she hadn't had a fresh kill lately. And the whole pick-a-date concept rubbed him the wrong way. He would decide when he went on a date with a woman, not some newspaper editor looking to increase readership with cheesy features.

But Mark was right. Warfield's needed the publicity. He'd throw Erin a bone and leave it at that. How difficult could it be?

Jared turned his attention to some paperwork without addressing that particular question. In his gut he knew he wouldn't like the answer.

Chapter Three

"Darn this stupid skirt," Erin muttered as she walked into the restaurant where she hoped to meet with Jared. While the skirt was attractive if she stood stock-still, every time she took a step the textured black material clung to her legs and crept higher. How did women get around in this sort of get-up? There was probably thigh glue or some kind of magical stuff to help with this irritating problem.

And, heavens, the push-up, padded bra Colleen had insisted Erin wear was doing its job—really well. The nasty, stiff thing was pushing up her chest into two mountain-like, unfamiliar structures under the tight, low-cut black stretch top she'd poured herself into. She actually had cleavage.

She stumbled, but managed to catch herself. While she supposed she looked good in the leather torture devices called shoes she'd jammed her feet into in the parking lot, who cared? If she fell on her face in the middle of the restaurant, no one would comment later that she'd looked darn good doing it.

This scheme had better be worth the hassle. She really needed to get her story and get on with her life, out from under the shadow of financial disaster.

She saw Jared in the far corner of the restaurant and relaxed a tad. At least he'd shown up, although she still had doubts about the interview. Jared Warfield seemed like one stubborn guy. But, boy, did he look like her dream date, even from a distance, sitting there all self-assured, his body angled to rest one arm on the back of his chair. His deep-blue, button-down shirt complemented his olive complexion and gave him a casual but successful look she found intriguing and extremely attractive.

His eyes followed her progress toward him, and she felt a feminine thrill at the appreciation glinting in their dark depths. She *did* look pretty good, didn't she? She pulled her shoulders back and thrust out her bra-enhanced chest the way Colleen had taught her, then swung her hips as she walked. Yeah, that was it, sway 'em, honey—

"Oof!" The sound popped from her mouth as she collided with a waiter. Before she could catch herself, her heel snagged on the carpet and she was teetering on the edge of a three-inch spike, desperately trying to stay upright. Somehow she managed to keep from falling on her butt. Barely. So much for the sexy routine.

Her face blazing, she looked at Jared and her hopes plummeted. The appreciative look had vanished, and his hand was over his mouth as mirth danced in his eyes. Had she blown her big plan already? Doubt hovered on the edge of her mind, eating away at her confidence in her ability to pull off this sexy act. She was way out of her league.

But humiliation was better than homelessness. She *had* to do this, so she kept walking.

Jared rose as she reached the table. He extended his hand. "Having a little trouble there?"

Erin shook his hand and his warm touch lit a fire under her skin. Dismayed, she managed to hold in a snappy comeback, remembering the interview. He was no dream date; this was strictly business. "I guess you could say that. My heel caught on the carpet."

His eyes flicked down briefly. "And your skirt? What did it catch on?"

Erin glanced down and gasped. Between the last tug and the table, her skirt had ridden almost all the way up her thighs. Only an inch or so saved her from total indecency. "Oh, my goodness!" She jerked the wayward garment down. "Darn the thing."

He smiled and raised an amused brow, but she thought him wise to keep silent. She unhitched the shoulder strap of her briefcase, put it down and plopped onto her chair. Her dignity had been left a few steps back, but she'd have to live with that. She had a job to do.

She looked at Jared. "Mr. Warfield—"

"Jared."

She nodded stiffly. While she *had* been thinking "stud-muffin" in her head, she wondered how smart it was to be on a first-name basis with him outside of her thoughts. Deciding not to worry about the small stuff, she said, "Jared, I'm so glad you decided to accept my invitation. To be honest, I wasn't sure you would."

His eyes still glinting with suppressed amusement, Jared took a sip of water. "I wouldn't have missed this for the world."

A tiny flare of irritation flashed through her. "What do you mean?"

He shrugged. "I wanted to find out how desperate you really were."

"But you're here for the interview, aren't you?"

He lifted a single brow. "Maybe I just came for a free lunch. Oh, and thanks for the book."

Ribbons of concern curled around Erin. This was a last-ditch effort, her one chance to save her financial bacon. She swallowed her concern and smiled the sexy, come-hither way she and Colleen had practiced in front of the mirror, remembering The Plan. "Oh, I have a feeling you'll cooperate."

He gave her a strange look, one she couldn't make sense of. She chose to read it as a positive sign.

"Are you all right?" he asked.

She held the smile and arched a brow. "Of course. Why do you ask?"

"Your face is all scrunched up and you have a tick in your eyebrow." He looked down and pressed his lips together. When he looked back up, he'd managed to wipe the smirk from his face. "Are you ill?"

Her smile faded and her eyebrow fell. Scrunched? A tick? That wasn't the effect she'd been going for. "Uh, no, not at all. I have something in my eye." She made a big show of rolling her eyes around.

"Need a tissue?" he asked, his tone appropriately serious.

She held up her hand. "No, I'm fine."

When she looked nervously back at him, he was studying his menu, a ghost of a smile hovering on his mouth. Her hopes sank again. She'd come here dressed like this to turn him on, not make him laugh. What had she been thinking? She knew better than to try to be something she wasn't, and this was hardly her. Plus, he was talking like he wasn't going to grant her the interview. Had she made a fool of herself for nothing?

She slanted another quick glance at him. When he

looked up, he caught her gaze with his heart-stopping, cocoa eyes. Then he smiled, flashing even, white teeth, and her blood warmed. He was just as gorgeous as she remembered, hang him. It would be ten times easier dealing with a man who didn't have the uncanny ability to turn her on by simply sitting there looking good. Horrified, she grabbed her menu and pretended to study it. The waiter arrived and they ordered, though she doubted she could eat a bite.

Despite the chaos whirling around inside of her like a child's toy top, it was time to get down to business. The direct approach seemed the way to go. Besides, she was too hot, bothered and worried for any more small talk.

She pushed up her glasses and opened her mouth to ask, once again, for his cooperation, but the words never made it past her lips.

Jared's pager trilled, and he looked down to his waist. "Sorry," he said, turning the device off. "I'll be right back." He excused himself, and Erin sat at the table alone, her stomach tied in knots, vaguely wondering why he didn't carry a cell phone.

Then her thoughts snagged on how busy Jared undoubtedly was. He would probably get called away on business and she'd lose the interview and she'd end up begging in the streets.

Sharp memories of her childhood rose in her, memories of the months she and her mother had spent on the razor edge of homelessness, the wolves of debt clawing at their door. Her breath left her in a rush. She couldn't live like that again. But she'd blown the interview a second time, and she hadn't uttered a word. Her crazy scheme had backfired and now he thought she was a scrunch-faced, tick-eyed fool in spike heels and a miniskirt.

A few tense minutes later, Jared returned from the front desk, his face neutral. No smile. No frown. Nothing.

Thoroughly deflated, Erin forced words past the tight lump in her throat. "No interview, right?"

He nodded tersely. "Right."

Her shoulders slumped. She pressed a hand to the base of her throat, fighting off tears.

"Hey, are you all right?" He sat back down.

She bit back a rueful laugh. He didn't really care whether or not she was okay. While keeping her heart safe from betrayal was necessary, it also left her alone with no one to turn to when things got tough.

"I'm fine," she whispered, lying.

And then she distinctly heard a wolf howling in the distance.

As a chill ran up her spine, she forced herself to look at Jared. His expression was still blank. He wasn't going to help her out.

Worse yet, she'd gone about getting this interview all wrong, stupidly alienating Jared from the start. Now she'd lost not only the best interview opportunity she'd had in months, but the chance to win the byline and bonus that could turn her life around.

Where did that leave her? Two steps closer to losing her home and everything she'd worked so hard for in the past two years.

And that was too darn close for comfort.

Erin's expression had fallen at Jared's news. Quite surprisingly he regretted he had to cancel the interview. It was probably because of how good she looked in that short skirt, tight top and heels, but he veered away from the thought, as if it had fangs. This wasn't the time or the place to let his hormones take over, even though she looked so good he wanted to reach under the table and see how short her skirt really was.

But business was business, and his was demanding attention. A vague sense of relief trickled through him. Now he could forget about this infernal interview, Allison would stay safe, and he could get away from Erin and the attraction that always seemed to take over every time he laid eyes on her.

He ignored the niggling voice in the back of his head, the one that sounded like Mark Phillips, chanting an ominous reminder about publicity. Canceling the interview couldn't be helped.

Erin looked up at him with those beautiful, grass-green eyes, now glassy with moisture. *Oh, man.* Near tears, she didn't look dangerous or like a cutthroat reporter. A heartbreaker, yes, but not a ruthless journalist.

Damn.

Was he being foolish and petty and overprotective of Allison? No thunderbolts would shoot from the sky and strike him dead if he gave the interview and suffered through one measly date. He was letting his past experience with the press cloud his normally clear judgment, and when it came to his business, he considered that akin to sinning. And he did feel guilty that Erin might lose her job if she didn't get this interview. She'd been as tenacious as a dog with a bone.

Yeah, he had to give her credit. She'd put it all on the line today to get the job done; her outfit had obviously been chosen to attract his attention, and, hot damn, it had worked. After all of her effort, she deserved the interview, although he told himself he wasn't giving in because he was attracted to her. He admired people who went to extremes to get what they wanted, and the interview would be good for business. Period. His fantasies about her would stay just that—fantasies.

He took a deep breath, wondering if he'd lost his mind. ''I've reconsidered, and I guess we could do the interview, after all.''

She gave him a slow, radiant smile. ''Oh, thank you!'' She grabbed his hand and squeezed.

Her touch felt like an electric shock.

She released his hand, and her gaze turned speculative. She leaned closer. ''Do you mind my asking why you changed your mind?''

Her rose scent washed over him, mixing with her sizzling touch to strike him dumb.

Before he could figure out how to respond, she said, ''No, don't tell me. I'm not about to press my luck. I'll consider this a divine gift and shut up. For once.''

He nodded, relieved. Obviously, he was overreacting. His attraction would stay firmly entrenched in his thoughts and dreams, which wouldn't threaten Allison. Or him.

Clearing his throat, he said, ''Fair enough. This is the deal. First off, no questions or comments about money. Second, I don't have any time today to do a formal interview. But you could spend the rest of the day with me and gather your information that way. I can answer questions, and you can have a personal glimpse into a typical day for me. How does that sound?''

She smiled again, and he couldn't help watching her sexy, plump lips. ''Great. When can we get started?''

He pulled his eyes from her mouth, determined to keep his physical reactions to her at bay. ''Right now. I've had a meeting moved up. We have to be in Beaverton in fifteen minutes.'' He laid some bills on the table.

Erin followed his lead and stood. ''Well, let's go, then,'' she said, turning. She began to wobble toward the door.

She was about six feet from him when he found his helpless gaze straying back to her legs. The breath left his body in a rush, and heat billowed through his gut when he noticed how far her skirt had ridden up. Fascinated, he watched her walk away.

Jared swallowed hard and forced himself to follow. He gave himself a quick, hard, mental shake. She was just an attractive woman. It was no big deal, right?

His mind whispered a feeble *right* back at him, and the pathetic response both mystified and concerned him. He hated not being able to control his feelings and physical reactions. He closed his eyes and shook his head in complete irritation.

Get over it. From now on, he'd ignore Erin's gorgeous body and concentrate on what had always been more important than emotional and physical entanglements—his family and his business.

Erin sat quietly in the passenger seat of Jared's car as he drove through Beaverton back to Portland.

Five hours and six appointments later, she realized she'd totally misjudged Jared Warfield. The man might be rich, but he was anything but lazy. He was hardworking, savvy, and remarkably astute when it came to his business.

Warfield's was expanding, and Jared was looking for locations for several new stores. They'd driven, walked— she thanked heaven she'd changed to flats—inspected and done the equivalent of kicking the tires on a car, but still they drove on to look at "just one more place." He'd forged ahead like a bulldozer, checking over every square inch of every possible site. He asked numerous questions, then stood and gazed and asked more and nearly drove the property agent nuts.

Erin had taken copious notes and had tried to keep her

mind on business. But it had been difficult. As soon as they'd climbed into his sports car, which she took great care not to comment on, and which, she noted, was conspicuously devoid of the baby seat, she'd realized they'd be sharing close quarters for the day. And while "up close and personal" was manna for her story, it was bad news for her body and her self-control. Jared was a very attractive guy, there was no doubt about it. Her feminine instincts seemed intimately attuned to every move he made.

"How'd you like to spy with me?" he asked, drawing her out of her musings. "I thought we might stop in at Java Joint and have a look at the competition."

"You actually do that? I mean, you actually go in and…spy?"

"Sure." He took a quick left, just making the light, and headed back toward Beaverton. "I like to know what my competitors are doing."

Erin's stomach growled. "Can we get something to eat?"

"You bet."

"Do I have to wear a disguise or something, you know like they did in *The Mod Squad?*"

He grinned and looked around surreptitiously, his face a study in mock seriousness. "Not today, but keep your wits about you. This coffeehouse spying can be pretty dangerous, you know."

She smiled, gave an okay signal and winked, helplessly drawn to this new, charming, playful side of Jared. "I understand. Let's go, then." As he negotiated the car around the block, she felt a tug at her heart, foolishly wishing she'd met Jared five years ago instead of Brent. Charming and playful were traits that were hard to ignore.

But she would. Brent's coldhearted treatment had taught

her how important it was for her to stay immune to any man, no matter how charming.

She would use this "coffeehouse spying" to ask Jared some more questions, specifically about his daughter. This was strictly business. Nothing more.

Five minutes later they pulled up to Java Joint, located in a pleasant, upscale mall in the heart of Beaverton. After they went inside and ordered, which took a long time because Jared kept changing his mind, they found a small table in the back and sat down.

Erin yanked on the lightweight black sweater she'd put on to cover her tight top and squirmed on the hard chair. "These chairs are awful."

Jared shifted. "Yeah, they are. That's why I've used a lot of couches and overstuffed chairs. People want to relax when they drink coffee, and relaxing on a chair like this is impossible. Everyone said I was crazy for putting fabric anywhere near so much hot, dark coffee—" He broke off and clamped his lips together. "Sorry. I get carried away when I talk shop."

"I don't mind at all. It tells me a lot about the kind of man you are." What it really told her was that he had his finger on the pulse of what the public wanted and that he was no lazy slouch. So very different from the man she'd originally thought he was.

His reply was precluded by the arrival of their coffee and their food, or in Erin's case, her dessert. She had a sweet tooth a mile long, despite her mother's lifelong desire to curb it.

"I wonder if they got this right." Jared took a quick swig of his coffee.

"Did you change your mind on purpose so many times when we ordered?"

He inclined his head. "Guilty. I wanted to see if they

could get the order right." He took another taste. "And they didn't."

"How about your staff? Have you tested them?"

"Of course. I have secret shoppers who come in and do stuff like this to test them. It keeps everybody on their toes."

"I'll bet." As much as Erin was enjoying the clever, ingenious side to Jared's personality, she had a few more questions to ask him. Reaching down, she dug her small tape recorder out of her bag. "I have a couple more things to ask you, and then we're done."

She turned on the small recorder. "So, I've asked all of the men I've interviewed what their idea of the perfect date is. How about yours?"

Jared paused, his hands steepled in front of his face. Erin anticipated his response with interest, knowing if he said anything about a vibrating bed (part of the last guy's answer), she'd probably retch, then be hugely relieved to shut down her body's need for a Jared-fest once and for all.

Finally, after what looked like some pretty serious consideration, he spoke. "My idea of the perfect date would be a leisurely drive down to the Oregon Coast. We'd stop in Cannon Beach and shop, then walk on the beach. After lunch at some cute little place, we'd buy salt-water taffy and fresh baked bread at the bakery. Then we'd go to Seaside and walk through town. We'd stop at the bumper cars, go for a spin on the merry-go-round, and go feed the sea lions at the aquarium. Then we'd find some nice, out-of-the-way seafood restaurant and have clam chowder, garlic bread and whatever else strikes our fancy. After dinner we'd drive home, exhausted and fat, but happy."

Erin sat as still as stone, her eyes down, stunned by what he'd said. If he'd read her mind, he couldn't have picked a more perfect response. The only thing she might add would be a long night at a cozy little bed-and-breakfast right on the beach. Provided, of course, that her date was Jared....

Whoa. This had to stop. She put a hand to her warm face, then clicked the recorder off. It was becoming obvious she couldn't trust her wayward imagination around him. She had to leave. Now. Before she made a fool of herself and he figured out what was running through her head. Time for a quick getaway.

But when she looked up, his dark, coffee-dusted gaze caught hers over his hands, and every instinct she had to leave flew right out the window. Her stomach fluttered, then flamed into a hot ball of need when she saw the unmistakable desire glowing in his eyes. Get out the straitjacket. He sent her senses spinning out of control with a simple story and a hot, smoldering look.

"How does that sound?" he asked, his voice deep, husky and compelling.

She grabbed the chain around her neck, cleared her throat and tried to speak. "Great," she finally managed to squeeze out. "Really nice." And then, because she was afraid she'd go into cardiac arrest, she tore her gaze from his and took a deep shuddering breath.

Desperately needing a distraction, she reached blindly for her coffee. She took a giant swallow, thankful it had cooled down enough not to burn her mouth. She eyed her chocolate éclair, but suddenly she wasn't in the least bit hungry. Her stomach was a mess, and she was a bundle of nerves. She'd never be able to choke down one bite.

Bad sign. Nothing affected her appetite. Ever. She'd put on ten pounds after Brent had left, still able to scarf down junk food with ease, despite her shattered heart and the stress of an unexpected, quickie divorce. She shook her head from side to side, wondering what in the world was wrong with her.

Like a flash of lightning reason returned. Her strange reaction didn't really matter. The interview was over, she had her story and hopefully the bonus. While her body obviously had a major thing for Jared Warfield, her brain knew better. Men were nothing but trouble. Another failure would be more than she could handle.

When she finally looked back up, Jared had dropped his eyes to study the small menu he'd picked up. It was time to make her exit, while she still had her dignity.

Her mind started working correctly again and she remembered his daughter. She wasn't going to walk away from another interview without asking him about her. "I have one more question."

"Shoot."

She swallowed and pushed up her glasses. "Uh...well, I noticed a baby car seat in your car the other day and did some research and discovered you adopted your niece."

He stared at her for a long time without moving, his warm, coffee gaze changing to mocha ice before her eyes. A muscle ticked in his granite-hard jaw. "I have no comment on that," he ground out, his lips barely moving.

A chill ran up her spine at his frosty, aloof answer, a cold shiver that was almost as disconcerting as the fire he'd lit in her blood just moments before. Hot, cold. What was wrong with her? Why did he have the frightening ability to bother her so much? And why was he so darn cagey?

Dreadfully uneasy at his mercurial change in attitude, and his wariness, she said the first thing that popped into her head. "I have to go."

"All right," he intoned.

Despite her reporter instincts screaming that the kid was a story, a story that might not only get her the bonus, but maybe even a raise, she stood, threw the recorder in her bag, yanked her skirt down and walked around his chair. Just a few yards and she'd be out of such close proximity and she could regain her equilibrium.

"Erin?"

She stopped. "Hmm?" She didn't quite trust herself to speak.

"You don't have a car. You came with me."

She almost groaned out loud. Swallowing hard, she smiled and nodded. "Of course. I knew that," she said, her voice high and tight. There would be no quick getaway, unless she took public transportation. Too bad she had no idea where the nearest bus stop was or how much the bus cost or even which bus to take. She was stuck with him.

Jared unfolded his long, lean body from the chair and stood, then gestured to the door. "After you."

Erin made her way to the door on shaking legs. Just fifteen more minutes and then she'd be fine.

Except that it was more like thirty minutes by the time they waited in the rush-hour traffic on the highway that ribboned through the West Hills from Beaverton to Portland. Jared turned on an oldies station, and they didn't talk much, which was good since her nerves and his nearness had suddenly affected her ability to speak coherently.

She was dying to ask him about his daughter, wondering why he was so reluctant to talk about her, but she sensed that subject was closed tight, and that piqued her interest even more.

As she sat next to him, she was acutely aware of the man beside her. His movements as he shifted gears were efficient, spare and somehow sexy. The sight of his big hands on the gearshift almost drove her wild. What was it about Jared behind the wheel of a fast, purring car that turned her blood to fire?

When he started to sing along with the radio, under his breath, Erin didn't know whether to be relieved or upset. The music helped cut some of the tension, but it also made Jared look, and sound, too appealing. He had a terrible voice, but he didn't seem to care. He sang softly, adding drumbeats against the steering wheel in typical male fashion.

Before long Erin relaxed and got into the music. When one of her favorites came on, she couldn't resist humming very, very softly under her breath. Humming didn't seem to do the song justice, and if she'd been alone, she would have been singing along at the top of her lungs. But she wasn't alone; Jared was sitting right next to her and she wouldn't dream of actually *singing* in front of him. She, too, had a terrible voice and no sense of rhythm.

Brent had always made fun of that.

She sneaked a peek at Jared, admiring his strong profile, liking the sound of his off-key singing. Before she could look away, he caught her studying him.

"What?" He looked at her from the corners of his cappuccino eyes. "You don't know the words?"

"I know the words—"

"Then sing along, chicken."

Oh-ho. She was no chicken. If Jared could "sing" then she could, as well. She hesitantly began to sing along, softly at first. But by the chorus she'd loosened up and was singing in earnest.

Jared knew the words, too, and they sang together, their voices clashing. The tension of mere minutes before vanished, and suddenly Erin felt more relaxed. But it didn't last long. The song ended, the news came on, and Jared flicked the radio off.

Dead silence reigned in the car. She searched her mind for something to say, but she was as tongue-tied as a schoolgirl on her first date. It was the second time in as many days that she'd found herself at a loss for words. Colleen would probably fall over in a dead faint. Erin's mom would thank the gods and hope it was a permanent affliction.

After what seemed like years Erin directed him to the lot where she always parked, and he stopped in the parking aisle behind her car. He put his car in neutral and turned toward her, leaning in. His arm snaked out to rest on the back of her seat. He wasn't too close, but close enough that she got a fresh whiff of him, mocha and cream mixed with the smell of man. She looked at her lap and studied the textured pattern on her skirt, hoping she could distract herself long enough to stay in control.

Her ploy failed miserably. Instead, she felt herself heading into a tailspin again. Her heart started pounding and her skin prickled in awareness. He was too close, too big and too darn good-looking. She put her hand on the door, keeping her eyes off him, but hesitated. She waited... heavens, for what?

And then he leaned closer, enclosing her even more with his broad body. She felt his dark eyes on her, studying her. She stared at the door handle, willing herself to pull it, open the door and leave. But she was unable to ease away from the pull of his blatant maleness or the possibility of what she might find in his arms. Peace? Contentment? An end to her loneliness? Whatever she might find, it would be heaven after Brent's callous behavior and her resulting emotional and physical isolation. She sensed an overwhelming connection between her and Jared, a connection she couldn't begin to understand.

She couldn't take it anymore. She had to know if he felt

the connection, too. She lifted her head and turned toward him.

The look in his dusky eyes yanked the breath from her chest like a quick, clever thief. Her body detonated when she dazedly realized he wanted her as much as she wanted him. She'd forgotten how good it felt to be the one person someone wanted more than anything. In fact, she didn't think she'd ever felt like this before. Certainly not with Brent...

Jared's big hand came up and lingered like a butterfly on her cheek. His simple touch set her ablaze.

"Jared..." She nuzzled his hand gently.

His fingers moved down and caressed her lips. "Your lips are like carnations. I've been wondering all day whether they're as soft and silky as they look."

"You have?" she whispered so softly she wasn't sure if he heard her.

He looked deeper into her eyes and moved so close she could see the umber flecks in his eyes. "I have. I want to kiss you to find out." Very slowly he removed her glasses and set them on the dashboard.

A hot thrill raced through her. She wanted his kiss more than her next breath. She clung to his probing gaze, unable to look or pull away. The thought of being in his arms filled her with a heady, eager anticipation she hadn't felt in forever. She was so sick of being alone, of isolating herself from feelings and emotions, for paying the terrible, painful price of Brent's profound failings, and hers, too.

His hand skimmed her cheek and moved to the back of her neck to burrow beneath her hair. She shuddered at the contact, nearly drowning in the sensation of being touched intimately by a man after so long. She let her eyes slide closed as she waited for his kiss. And then his mouth touched hers.

Erin groaned, lost. Her resolve to keep her distance completely faded away. His lips were moist, warm and incredibly gentle. The kiss started softly; he skimmed her lips with his, tasting and teasing lightly. But it wasn't enough, not nearly enough, and he seemed to sense that right away. Just as she twined one hand up to the back of his head to pull him closer, he made a low, dark sound in the back of his throat and slanted his mouth fully on hers. Erin shifted, and suddenly her mouth was open and she felt his tongue touch hers.

Long-forgotten desire spilled through her like water from a broken dam. She stroked her tongue into his mouth, tasting coffee and whipped cream and him.

He raised his head, but she wasn't ready to relinquish the touch of his lips. She'd denied herself too long to let their kiss end yet. Just another kiss…

"Don't stop," she gasped, pulling his mouth back to hers.

He took her mouth again, and their kisses turned wild and uncontrolled. Leaning back, she pulled him down to lie half on top of her. She felt his hands move around from her back to her waist. He seemed to know what she needed and wanted and was ready to give it to her, which blew her mind. For as long as she could remember, no one had cared about her wants and needs—only their own.

"Erin, honey," he rasped against her mouth, his tongue caressing her lips. "Let's go—"

Hoooooonnnnnnnnk!

Ice water poured through her veins.

Jared shot up, breathing heavily, and jerked his head around, glaring at the car behind them. He turned toward the steering wheel, shoved the stick into first and gunned the engine. The car jumped ahead, its tires squealing, and

Erin flew forward and caught herself against the dashboard with her hands as he moved the car to unblock the aisle.

Erin pushed back against the seat and slouched down as the other car drove by. What had she been thinking? Where was her control? Mortified, she put her hands over her face and prayed for the ability to snuff out the startling, undeniable desire Jared had awakened in her.

"Man, I completely forgot where we were," he admitted after he'd pulled into a space slightly down from Erin's car.

Her heart pounding, she took a deep breath, thrown completely off-kilter by their sizzling kiss and by how right it had felt to be locked in his arms. "Yeah, me, too."

He hunched over the steering wheel, then turned and looked at her. His eyes, now as black as burned coffee, still glowed with desire and need. She wanted to yank him back to her and finish their kiss, but she couldn't get herself in any deeper than she already was. This was all wrong. A relationship meant too much heartache when it didn't work out, and she was sure he would never want plain old her for long. Her father hadn't loved her enough to stay alive, and Brent sure hadn't cared about her, either. Already Jared was keeping secrets. It would be best to take another deep breath and walk away from him. For good.

She briefly grasped the chain around her neck, then darted her gaze away, gathering the strength to leave. She reached for her glasses. "Well, thanks for the interview and for bringing me to my car."

He nodded. "You're welcome."

She slipped her glasses on, opened the door and climbed out, not trusting herself to look at him again. She slammed the door, then looked through the partially open window, taking great care to look past his shoulder and not in his eyes, which always seemed to strike her dumb. No, she didn't trust herself around this man at all, and it would be too easy to lose herself to him, just as she'd lost herself to Brent. After a while she'd disappeared, and it had taken a long, long time to find herself again. She wouldn't take that risk a second time.

"Maybe I'll call you or something," he said.

She held her hands up and shook her head. "No, I...uh, please don't," she said, her face heating.

He gave a quick, terse nod.

Taking heed of her underused brain cells, she turned on her heel and walked away, her knees shaking. As soon as she got in her car, she'd be fine.

But once she unlocked her car and gave in to her shaking legs and sat down, instead of feeling fine she only felt lonely and empty and somehow incomplete.

Definitely not what she was hoping for.

Chapter Four

Erin returned from having lunch with her mom and flopped into her chair behind her desk. She looked at Colleen. "Why do I always do this?"

"Do what?"

"Let my mom do her usual number on me. I always swear I'm not going to let her get to me, and lately, because she's been making noise about things being different between us, I thought everything would be okay." She sighed and rubbed her throbbing temple. "But nothing's changed. She still makes me feel like an inadequate little girl. Boy, do I wish she wasn't spending the night." Her mom lived an hour from Portland in a little town close to the coast, but made the trip to Portland a few times a month for shopping and appointments.

"You want me to drop-kick her for you?"

Erin smiled and opened her desk drawer in search of some pain reliever. "As tempting as that thought is, no. On some small level, she does seem to be making the effort, especially since her new husband left her. I'm sure she must feel very alone, and despite how she always belittles me, she *is* my mom.''

Colleen flipped her curly blond hair behind her ear. ''Well, if you change your mind, let me know.'' She looked up, a speculative gleam lighting her blue eyes. ''So, when do you get to interview Jared and his date?''

Erin glared at Colleen, sick of her incessant prodding about Jared. ''I don't *get* to interview them, Joe's *making* me do this follow-up. And I'd appreciate it if you would just lay off about Jared.'' She opened the bottle of pain reliever and shook two tablets into her hand.

''After you guys kissed in his car?'' Colleen snickered. ''I don't think so. I haven't had something this juicy on you in a long time. You're a female monk—''

''Nun,'' Erin supplied. ''That would make me a nun.''

''Whatever. You live like a nun, and suddenly you tell me you've been mashing peas with your latest interviewee. This is too good to pass up.''

Erin snorted, wished a pox on Colleen and wondered what had ever possessed her to confide in her friend. Erin had made a big show of minimizing what had happened with Jared, but deep down, she was a mass of confusion. In the three weeks since she'd completed the interview and the story, she'd been a closet basket case.

And now she would have to face Jared and the woman Joe had picked from the hundreds who had written in, hoping for a chance to snag a millionaire. Jared had reluctantly agreed to go on the date, and now it was time for Erin to do her part and find out how the date went and whether they'd be seeing each other again, and write about it.

At least she'd been awarded the byline and bonus for her version of ''The Bachelor Chronicles.'' The bonus had taken care of most of Brent's outstanding credit card balances, which left her with enough money to make her mortgage payments. She was still on a tight budget, but she wasn't looking foreclosure in the eye any longer. But for how long?

She checked her watch. She couldn't put off seeing Jared any longer. She just wanted to get it over with so she could forget the cute-guy-daddy-dog-lover for good, although, as the days went by, she was growing more and more curious about Jared's daughter and why he'd refused to talk about the little girl.

With a sense of impending doom, she stood, swilled down the pills with a drink from the bottle of water she kept on her desk, grabbed her bag and dolefully looked at Colleen. "I gotta go."

"Geez, cheer up. You're going to an interview, not an execution."

Erin straightened, tugged her bag up onto her shoulder and smiled brightly, a lot more brightly than she felt. "There, is that better?"

"Much." A significant pause. "Just don't kill her."

"What is that supposed to mean?" Erin asked, though she already had a pretty good idea.

"You know. Don't kill Jared's date."

Erin frowned. "Why would I want to do that?"

"Do you think I'm an absolute idiot?"

"Ye—"

"Don't answer that. My point is, you and Jared kissed, and we're talking a big, deep, serious kiss here. And you're jealous." Colleen held up her hands and curled her fingers as if she had claws. "Try to keep your claws from showing."

Though Colleen had come darn close to the truth, Erin would never admit it out loud. This infatuation she had for

Jared had to stop, and as soon as she finished the story, it would. "I am not jealous of anybody," she lied. "Really."

"Right. Whatever you say."

Erin couldn't round up the energy to get into it again with Colleen, especially since her friend was dead-on. Instead, Erin sighed and turned to go.

"Oh, by the way," Colleen called as Erin reached the door. "Did I mention Luke brought up the proofs for the pictures he took of all the bachelors and their dates?"

Erin jerked her head around. "He did? Where?" She hurried over to Colleen's desk, her hand held out.

Colleen held out a single proof. "Here you go."

With eager hands Erin reached out and took the lone picture, praying the woman was ugly. She knew she was being uncharitable and downright mean, but she couldn't seem to help it. *She* wanted to be the center of Jared's universe—theoretically, of course. In the real world she couldn't let a man that close.

She looked at the picture. Her shoulder bag fell to the floor with a *clump.* Her heart plummeted, and jealousy crawled through her with all the grace of a fat, hungry rat.

The woman was beautiful. Short and petite, she had luxuriously smooth, long, dark hair, creamy olive skin and almond-shaped brown eyes. She was everything Erin never would be.

Gorgeous. Petite. Having a good hair day.

Erin had always been too tall, too gawky and just plain too big. Erin's unruly red hair had been the bane of her mother's existence from the moment Erin had been born. A day hadn't gone by when she hadn't heard about "that mop of hair."

She stood stock-still, wishing she was different, wishing she could have pleased everyone in her life. But she'd been down that road a thousand times, and it always led absolutely nowhere, except into Brent's arms. Same road, different person. Lesson learned. She was who she was.

"Erin, are you all right?" Colleen asked.

Erin forced her painful thoughts away. "I'm fine." She handed the picture back to Colleen and shoved her inadequate feelings aside, suddenly determined not to let the woman in the picture bother her. Jared meant nothing to her. Well, okay, he was the stuff dreams were made of, but she didn't want to dream anymore. He was free to date anybody he wanted to.

"Thanks for trying to make me feel better," she told Colleen. "But I'm okay with this whole thing. Once this story is done, I'll probably never see him again."

"Do you want to see him again?"

Colleen's serious question caught her off guard. She was dismayed to admit to herself that she wanted him, but she didn't go for casual sex. And a relationship was impossible. She'd failed once. Enough said.

Determined to minimize her attraction to Jared, both to herself and her nosy friend, she replied, "No, I don't want to see him again. I've sworn off men for good, you know that."

"But this is Jared Warfield," Colleen pointed out. "Guys like him come along once—"

Erin ruthlessly cut her off. "I gotta run." She headed toward the door, unwilling to listen to Colleen's rundown of why Jared was such a catch. She was thoroughly aware of why he was so darn desirable. "See you tomorrow."

"Fine." Colleen flicked her fingers in the air. "Run away. But there's more to this than meets the eye."

Erin waved and kept going. Colleen was attracted to anything in pants and had loads of experience with men. But she was dead wrong about this. There was nothing more to this situation than raging, out-of-control hormones. And hormones were something Erin could handle.

She'd gather her control, write the final article in "The Bachelor Chronicles" series, and forget the way Jared's lips had pressed against hers and the way she'd felt as if she belonged in his arms and the way she'd dreamed of him cuddling his daughter close.

And that would be the end of it.

She hoped.

"Stay down. Doggie? Stay."

Vaguely irritated, Jared watched Hilary try to keep Josie from jumping on her. The woman obviously didn't like animals; she'd spent the better part of their "date" shooing Josie away.

An afternoon that couldn't end soon enough as far as he was concerned. He'd grudgingly agreed to this date simply because it meant more publicity, and though Hilary wasn't mean or petty or anything else overtly bad, she was…weird. After several graphic stories about the emergency room where she worked as a nurse, an offer to read his destiny with her tarot cards, and a pointed reference to the spaceships that were supposed to land on the Oregon Coast next month, he could see she was a little on the strange side.

Instead of being interested in Hilary, his mind was on Erin. He'd thought a lot about her since they'd kissed in his car, which had given him a new perspective on what *uncontrollable physical attraction* meant. He still hadn't managed to get the sight of her in that tiny black skirt out of his mind, or the way she'd felt, so soft and feminine, in his arms.

But he'd honored her wishes and hadn't called, which he knew was best. Erin had already figured out he had a daughter, and he just couldn't ignore his desire to protect Allison from the press. But he'd been tempted to call Erin. Really tempted. The memories of her curvy body against his haunted him, leaving him frustrated and short-tempered. And, man, he really liked her, too. She was stubbornly, naturally unpretentious, and had a huge soft spot for Josie, which earned her extra points.

He figured seeing her today would prove that his attraction was a fluke, not something that really mattered or something he couldn't easily control.

He suddenly spied the subject of his thoughts.

Erin.

His heart jumped, and a huge bubble of anticipation burst in his chest, making him wonder about his attraction being a fluke. Erin looked like a ray of sunshine dressed in loose-fitting yellow pants and a flowered vest with a yellow shirt underneath it. Her auburn curls glinted like fire in the afternoon sun, contrasting vividly with her ivory complexion and carnation-kissed lips. She looked fantastic.

She drew near, and he willed his pulse to slow down. She was here to finish her story, nothing more. He had to remember that and not get carried away with how pretty she looked or with how much he liked her. In the long run, a pretty woman and warm, fuzzy feelings didn't matter. Walking away from Erin after this interview and protecting Allison *did* matter.

"Hey, you two," Erin called, waving. "What a great spot for a picnic."

Josie bounded over and yipped in greeting. Erin squatted down and caught the squirming mass of puppy in her arms. A lot of puppy kisses followed, which Erin bore with good grace.

Jared smiled, liking Erin's relaxed attitude, and heard Hilary sniff in disgust.

Erin picked Josie up and walked toward them. "Sorry to interrupt this, but I have to ask a few questions. After that you can go back to your date."

Jared bit his tongue. It would be impolite to tell Erin he'd rather that *she* stayed to be his date. "No problem. Erin, this is Hilary McCall. Hilary, this is Erin James from the *Beacon*. She'll be doing the follow-up interview."

Hilary nodded and smiled. "Nice to meet you, Erin."

Erin sat on a corner of the blanket, seemingly as far from him as she could get, then plopped Josie on the ground and started rummaging through her bag. Josie crawled onto Erin's lap where she curled up and put her head on her paws. They looked so cute together Jared fought the urge to move closer. He jerked on his watch and forced himself to remember that Erin wasn't here to cozy up, and that was the way he wanted it.

"Ah, here we go," Erin said, pulling out her tape recorder. "I promise this won't take long."

Jared watched Erin fiddle with the machine, wondering why she hadn't met his gaze yet. He'd hoped for one of her shy smiles and a glimpse of her gorgeous eyes. That was innocent enough. But she appeared to be all business.

He gave a mental snort. What did he expect? She was here for her job. Period. Yet he wondered if he leaned in close would she still smell like roses…?

When Erin got the tape recorder working and clicked it on, he thudded back to reality.

She looked at Hilary first. "So, Hilary, tell me about your date."

"Well, it really wasn't much. We just met for this… 'picnic.' And he brought *her* along," Hilary nodded tersely toward Josie, "so it's been hard to do much of anything, let alone talk."

Jared suppressed a wry smile. Hilary had done plenty

of talking in between complaints about Josie. Though he'd been polite, he just wasn't interested in anything she had to say. And she certainly hadn't seemed particularly interested in him, except for where he lived and what kind of car he drove. Plus, she'd actually hit him up for a donation to the Society for the Cosmically Aware. He'd seen it all before, those dollar signs in a woman's eyes. It was doubly bad that she was downright weird.

"You don't like dogs?" Erin asked Hilary.

Hilary wrinkled her nose. "No. All the hair and slobber…yuck. It throws my *chi* way out of balance."

"So you aren't interested in snagging a millionaire?" Erin bluntly asked.

"I'm only interested in being with a man who is in tune with the cosmos." Hilary pushed Josie away and shook her head. "Jared doesn't even know what the cosmos is."

Erin turned and looked at him. Her leafy eyes glinted with amusement, and her mouth was pressed into a tiny, secretive grin. "Jared, why a picnic? Why not something more…intimate, like say, a trip to the beach and a romantic dinner?"

He raised a brow, wondering why she was bringing up his perfect date scenario. Was she mocking him, or was she really interested? Probably neither. She was only concerned with writing an interesting story, not with really knowing him.

"I'm a down-to-earth kind of guy. Besides, it's a beautiful day. I thought a picnic would be a nice change." He didn't add that an intimate, expensive dinner, which most women expected from him, was out of the question for that very reason. To go even further, his dream date was reserved for his fantasy woman, the nonexistent one who would love him without strings attached, not some weird female who would probably go searching for alien space-craft if he took her anywhere near the Oregon Coast.

Erin gave him a speculative, inquiring look. "So, what was the most fascinating thing you discovered about Hilary?"

Oh, man, help him come up with something to say. *Strange* hardly classified as fascinating. "Uh, well, let's see." He rubbed his chin. "She likes tarot cards and Martians?"

Erin grinned. "Are you asking me or telling me?"

Her smile hit him in the gut like a two-by-four. "Uh…telling you. Hilary likes tarot cards and Martians. Oh, yeah. And she once lanced a boil on Dalton Marx's…uh, rear end."

Erin stilled and here eyes grew wide. She glanced over at Hilary. "Ah. I see." She pressed her mouth together tightly and ducked her head. He could tell she wanted to laugh. When she looked back up, her eyes were twinkling with suppressed mirth. "Who is Dalton Marx?"

Hilary cut in. "He's the leading authority on Martian spacecraft sightings and abductions in Oregon." She rolled her eyes. "Jeez, don't you guys keep up on extraterrestrial visitation?"

"Nope," Jared said.

"Me, neither," Erin added.

Damn. One more reason to like Erin.

Erin threw him a conspiratorial smile, but before she could ask her next question, a large dog came bounding by. Josie leaped to her feet, barking up a storm. In a flash she was off, chasing the other dog up and over the slight rise behind them.

Jared sprang to his feet. "Hey! Josie! Come back here."

He took off after the two dogs, suddenly grateful for the break. What could be worse than rehashing a boring date to a woman who seemed a hell of a lot more interesting than the date herself, while said date was sitting there listening? He didn't want to like Erin, but he did.

He chased Josie and the other dog around a couple of large trees and through a large patch of mud, which Jared managed to avoid. Somewhere along the line, Josie lost interest and headed back to their picnic spot.

Just as Jared crested the rise to return to Hilary and Erin, he heard a loud shriek. He looked down and nearly laughed out loud. Hilary, her arms thrown wide, stood with a horrified, indignant expression on her face. Josie was dancing at Hilary's feet, barking merrily. Obviously, the naughty puppy had jumped all over his "date." Muddy paw prints decorated Hilary's cream-colored pants and pink blouse. Her immaculate outfit was a muddy mess. Oh, boy.

"You bad, bad dog!" she shrieked, flailing her arms.

Erin grabbed Josie and picked the excited puppy up, heedless of the mud on Josie's paws. "I've got her."

Hilary glared at Jared and flung her hands down to gesture impatiently at her clothes. "Look what that stupid mutt did."

Jared swallowed a laugh and did his best to look contrite. "I...I'm sorry. Here." He pulled out his wallet and peeled off a couple of bills. "Take this and have your clothes cleaned. But you'd better go right away. Before the mud sets, that is."

Hilary grabbed the cash as he knew she would. "Fine with me. I've had enough puppy slobber and mud to last me a lifetime." Muttering under her breath, she gathered up her things and stomped off, calling over her shoulder, "And, Jared, please don't call me. You're really not my type. I saw it in the cards days ago but ignored it." She flounced off, unaware of the brown paw print Josie had somehow managed to plant right in the middle of her fanny.

Once she was out of sight, Jared turned and looked at Erin. She held Josie in one arm and she had her other hand over her mouth to hold in a laugh.

"What a mess." He clenched his lips together to keep from laughing. "It would be mean to laugh."

Erin nodded, then snorted behind her hand. "Yeah... really mean."

He bit his lip hard, but a chortle popped from his mouth. Then a snicker. Then a full-fledged guffaw. It might be mean, but the sight of Hilary with a muddy paw print in the middle of her butt struck him as hilarious.

Erin giggled behind her hand, then wholeheartedly joined in. They both hooted uproariously together until his sides hurt. He liked the sound of her laughter, all throaty and rich and real, and he liked letting loose with her. A strange feeling settled over him, and it took a second for him to recognize what the sensation was. Contentment. Yeah, he felt content and happy.

His laughter faded, and he tried to remember when a woman had ever made him feel like this. He'd deliberately kept all women at arm's length, not wanting to repeat his father's mistakes and let a woman take advantage or risk an emotional entanglement that might hurt Allison. But he instinctively sensed that the contentment stealing over him was tied up in the beautiful woman seated next to him, muddy paw prints decorating her clothes. He might not really like the idea, especially since Erin was a reporter, but it was hard to deny how much he liked being with her. He decided to quit analyzing himself and simply enjoy himself. An afternoon at the park seemed harmless enough.

She flipped up her glasses to rest them on top of her head, rubbed a hand across her watery eyes and put Josie down. "Martians? Boils? Anything else I should know? For the article, I mean."

He shook his head. "I think that about covers it," he replied, sinking down onto the blanket. He looked at her flowered vest, which was smeared with mud. "Oh, man, I'm sorry about your clothes."

Erin looked down and shrugged, then sat down, closer this time. "Big deal. It's just mud. It'll wash out."

He reached for his wallet. "Here—"

She gave him a disparaging look and put her glasses back on. "Please, put the wallet away. I don't want your money."

Jared pulled his hand away from his pocket and winced inwardly, feeling like a heel for offering at all. He was just so used to women having their hands out, he'd expected the same of her.

Thrown momentarily off balance, he reached over and opened the wicker picnic basket. "Hungry? I have plenty of greasy fried chicken and jo-joe potatoes left."

She looked away and bit her lip. "I don't know...." She ran a hand through her hair. "I really should be going. I asked Hilary some more questions while you were chasing Josie, but I'm going to have to rack my brain to come up with a good piece."

"Oh, come on," he coaxed. "It's really tasty." He picked up a drumstick and took a big bite. "Yum."

She stared at him. "Hitting me where I live, huh?"

"What do you mean?"

She waved a hand in the air, then smiled that little smile of hers, that shy curving of her lush mouth he loved. "Just that I like to eat, much to my mother's chagrin. She once told me, in front of the whole neighborhood, that my appetite put a trucker to shame."

He had a hard time believing that, especially after he'd

gotten a look at her long, slim legs. "Believe me, you don't look like a trucker."

She inclined her head. Her hair fell forward in a shimmering red-gold mass of curls. "Why, thank you, kind sir." She flashed him a bright grin. "You've made my day."

His mouth went dry. Man, that killer smile never failed to knock him senseless. "Glad I could oblige." Fighting the urge to reach out for her, he held up a piece of chicken instead. "Now, how about it?"

She hesitated, one delicately curved brow raised, her eyes glinting like sun-warmed moss. Her small grin grew into a dazzling smile. "All right. But just one piece."

Pleased and nearly knocked off his feet again by her smile, Jared handed her the piece of chicken on a paper plate. "Oh, wait, you have to have the jo-joes. No picnic is complete without them."

She accepted the fried potato slices, then dug in to her food with gusto, clearly enjoying every bite. "So, I guess you won't be seeing Hilary again."

He gave her a sly, teasing look. "Interested, now, are you?" he asked, warming up to a little innocent flirting.

She stopped chewing and looked at him, then blinked. "Uh, no. I just need to know for the article. The readers will want to know for sure about that."

He nodded and looked right in her eyes, curious about whether there was more than her job keeping her here. "Mmm-hmm. And there's no personal interest there at all?" He certainly hadn't imagined her returning his kiss in the car.

She paused and stared back, unblinking. As quick and as bright as lightning, something passed between them, something electrifying. His stomach lurched, and desire hummed to life inside of him. He wanted to reach out and pull her to him and kiss those carnation-petal lips. But she'd probably take off the way she had after their last kiss, and he wanted to enjoy her company before they went their separate ways.

Because after they ate, he *would* walk away. He had Allison to think of now. A reporter could be bad news for his family, and Erin had already discovered he had a daughter. He wasn't about to risk his heart on a woman who might use him. Even knowing that, he couldn't seem to fight this insane desire to pull Erin close and lose himself in the elusive happiness warming him now.

Back up, Warfield. This ended today. He and Erin would share a few pieces of chicken and some light conversation and then they'd go their separate ways. That way he'd stay safe. Simple as that.

"Good enough," he said, striving to keep his tone light. "It keeps things simple."

And it would be simple. Today only. Nothing more. Because after his father's disastrous love life and because of Allison, that was all Jared would allow.

Chapter Five

It was a warm, blue-skied, picture-perfect day. Hilary was gone and had taken her muddy pants and Martians with her. And best of all, Erin had charming, intriguing, Jared Warfield all to her little-old self. Maybe she should pinch herself and wake up from this fantasy.

But she wouldn't. It wouldn't hurt to relax and take pleasure in Jared for an hour or two before she never saw him again. There was no harm in enjoying an innocent, casual picnic—even with Brent's betrayal constantly hovering in the back of her mind, an aching reminder she could never ignore.

Still, she was determined to enjoy this brief picnic. Sighing in pleasure, she flopped back on the blanket, her appetite thoroughly satisfied. "That was the best chicken I've had in years."

"It's my secret recipe," Jared said, his cocoa eyes looking heavenly next to the cream-colored polo shirt he wore. "Glad you liked it."

"No way." She sat back up. "You cook, too?"

Smiling, he nodded. "Sure. I've even been known to do my own laundry."

He did laundry? *Be still my heart.* Brent hadn't even managed to pick his dirty clothes off the floor. "So did you make this whole meal?" Erin gestured to the picnic basket.

"Everything but the jo-joes. I've never been able to get the seasoning right—"

"But you've tried to make them?"

"Sure. I make it a point to try to make all the foods I really like."

Erin was very impressed. She could barely boil water without burning it, and the closest Brent had ever come to the kitchen was when he walked by it in the morning. "Do you cook a lot?"

"Not as much as I'd like to."

Erin shook her head and laid back down, telling herself Jared couldn't be as perfect as he seemed. No man was.

He smiled crookedly, then looked off in the distance, propping an elbow on his jean-clad, raised knee. "I've been wanting to call you, but I didn't because you said not to."

Her stomach flip-flopped, and a deep, totally ridiculous sense of pleasure rolled through her. She took a calming breath and then ruthlessly crushed her happiness. His admission didn't matter. After today Jared would be nothing but a guy she'd interviewed for a story.

He picked up a curl of her hair. "It's obvious I'm attracted to you, and I think you feel the same about me...."

Major understatement.

She let him trail off and watched his fingers lightly toy with her hair, her breath caught in her throat, her heart thumping. She should pull away and run as fast as she could. Jared was hiding things she ought to ask about instead of kissing him, and she was dead sure he had the power to hurt her. But she was frozen in place by how much she liked his gentleness and simple tastes, not to mention how attracted she was to him physically—and that it was mutual.

Keeping this picnic impersonal was impossible with Jared turning on the charm. She wanted to know everything about him. She wanted his hands on more than her hair. She wanted him everywhere.

A light breeze stirred her pant legs. Birds twittered in the trees and a lawn mower buzzed in the distance. Her heart kept pumping wildly in her chest, as if she'd run a long, long way. Excitement skittered under her skin like millions of tiny arrows.

And then he looked down, directly at her. Those deep, espresso-hued eyes pinned her to the ground, and she felt her stomach clench and tighten with need. Her heart almost exploded.

He ran his hand through her hair. "I've wanted to do this since I first saw you."

His gaze trailed to her mouth and lingered. Her breath stilled at the way he stared at her lips and at the feel of his hands in her hair. All thoughts of running away from this wonderful man vanished instantly. She couldn't move a muscle, much less deny herself the wonder of his kiss.

Just one, teensy kiss…

"Erin," he murmured huskily, leaning over her. "Tell me to stop, honey, because I'm going to kiss you."

She tried to say something, but nothing came out…only a tiny, muffled sigh. They were in a public park. What could happen? It was a simple kiss, nothing to be afraid of, really, and oh, how she wanted his mouth on hers again. She'd been alone for so long….

He loomed closer and closer as his head dropped toward

her. He removed her glasses and set them on the blanket, and his now-familiar scent, coffee and him, teased her nose. Her eyes drifted shut, and then, just when she thought she'd come out of her skin in anticipation and need, his mouth claimed hers.

Oh, yes!

He wasted no time on preliminaries. The kiss was hot and deep from the start. She opened her mouth and welcomed his tongue in with a hungry groan, then pulled him closer with trembling arms. Her will to resist flooded out of her in a rush, leaving her hot and shaking and wanting more and more.

His hands drifted over her ribs, then moved up to skim lightly over her breasts. She gasped at the rasp of his fingers though her shirt.

He pulled away, then trailed kisses down her cheek and into the valley of her neck. "Honey, you smell so good. I want you...."

No one had wanted her like this in a very long time, maybe never. Filled with a desperate longing and a heady power, she arched into him as he nuzzled her neck, kissing and licking, while she trailed eager hands over his taut, muscled back and shoulders. She could spend hours exploring his body, losing herself in every sculpted muscle, every bit of male flesh that was so different from her own....

A whine echoed close to her ear and then a wet tongue licked at her face. And it sure wasn't Jared...*Josie.*

Jared pulled away, kicking up one corner of his mouth. "Hold that kiss, Erin."

He pushed to a sitting position, picked up Josie and cuddled her close. "Josie-girl, are you jealous? Do you need some attention?" He ran his big hands over the tiny white fluffball and scratched her behind her little ears.

Thoroughly entranced, Erin watched him shower an adoring Josie with attention, attention Josie would be guaranteed for as long as she wanted it. What a lucky dog.

And Erin?

Oh, he will break my heart for sure.

Reality tumbled down on her like a load of bricks. This had to stop. Right now. She wasn't about to repeat history and jump into a relationship. The wound on her heart would make sure of that.

Jared put Josie down, then instantly reached for Erin again.

She scooted back on the blanket, determined to keep some distance now. "Jared...no." She sucked in a shaky breath.

He ran a hand through his short hair. "Yeah, I guess you're right. I seem to forget myself when you're around." He started loading the picnic basket. "Man, what in the world is wrong with me?"

Her heart ached. Did he think it was wrong to want her? She closed her eyes, willing her senses, and body, back to normal and tried to ignore the hurt his words had caused. "And me. I've told myself you're off-limits, but I keep forgetting."

He gave a humorless laugh. "Off-limits? That's pretty harsh."

Harsh? Maybe. But necessary. She'd never survive another heartbreak. "I...uh, haven't had much luck in the man department," she explained. "I have a habit of picking the wrong guys."

"And I'm wrong?"

"With a capital *W,*" she mumbled. Granted, he seemed totally different from Brent. But getting tangled up with Jared would only lead to hurt.

"What?" he asked.

"Yes," she whispered. "You are."

His eyes slid away, and a muscle jumped in his jaw. He dumped the paper plates into a plastic bag. "Why?"

Erin sat up and grasped the chain around her neck. "Jared, I don't want to become involved with anyone. My ex-husband hurt me. I caught him in bed with one of my friends, and he left me with a ton of bills, and well...I can't go through that again. Not ever."

His mouth formed a grim line. "What a jerk."

"Yeah, well, that's one way of putting it." She reached for her glasses, put them on, then picked Josie up.

"I know what it's like to be hurt." His gaze skittered away briefly. "Maybe we could take it...slow."

She raised her brows and studied him, wondering what hurt a man like him. But she shoved those thoughts aside to focus on what she was trying to tell him. Taking things slowly wouldn't change the fact that she wouldn't let herself get involved with or risk loving a man again.

"Do you want a serious relationship right now?" she asked, coming at the problem from a different direction. "Be honest."

He adjusted his watch on his arm. "No." He reached out to pet Josie. "That's my loss," he murmured, vague regret shadowed in his eyes. "And yours. It could have been good between us, Erin."

He tipped her chin up and kissed her again, plying her lips open and sweeping her mouth with his warm, hot tongue. She clung to his hungry kiss, wishing she could let herself care for this warm, funny guy.

But that was just a dream.

He abruptly pulled away and looked deep in her eyes. "Damn good."

He rolled to his feet, took Josie from her, picked up the picnic basket and bag of garbage, and left Erin with her lips pulsing from his kiss and his promise-filled words echoing in her head.

Damn good was right.

"Stupid car," Erin muttered, drumming her fingertips on the steering wheel.

Jared's head popped up over the open hood of her junker. "Try it again."

She turned the key, but nothing happened. Not a click. Not a sputter. Nothing. It was as dead as a frozen side of beef.

He walked around to the driver's window. "Looks like it's the battery. I'll jump you—"

She smirked and snorted. *I wish.*

"You better watch it, missy, or I *will* jump you." His eyes held a promise she wished she could take him up on.

"Oooooh, I'm scared," she mock whimpered.

He arched a dark brow and shot her a look that sent her stomach tumbling. "You oughta be. Anyway, my guess is you need a new battery." He cast a disparaging glance toward her dented, ancient heap of a car. "And a new car."

"Yeah, I know. But the mortgage comes first. Go ahead and use the cables."

Five minutes later, even after they'd attached the jumper cables and poured enough power from Jared's car into Erin's to light a small city, the car was still dead.

He shook his head. "Yeah, you either need a new battery or a new alternator."

She got out of the car and kicked a tire in fury. "I'll have to have it fixed." She hoped whatever she needed was cheap, because she barely had enough money in her checking account to cover necessities.

"Don't worry. I'll take you home and arrange for a tow truck."

She didn't like the sound of that. She needed to get away from his hot glances, heart-stopping kisses and charming personality. Her willpower was seeping out of her like a Popsicle left in the sun. There had to be another way.

"Do you have a cell phone?" she asked.

"Nope."

She gave him an incredulous look. "Why not? Doesn't every successful guy have one?"

"Not this one. Too much of a distraction." He dug in his pocket and held up a pager. "My assistant can reach me if necessary."

"Darn it." She nibbled a nail.

"Don't you have a cell phone?"

"Um…the battery ran down a few days ago, and I never recharged it." She was too embarrassed to tell him that a cell phone was a luxury she couldn't afford right now. Even though she'd paid off the majority of Brent's bills with her bonus, she was still on a budget tighter than shoes two sizes too small.

She was stuck. "All right. You can take me home." She sent up a silent prayer for strength and control. Every minute she spent with him weakened her resolve to keep him at arm's length.

As they drove to her house, Jared chatted amiably about all kinds of inane things like the movies he'd seen recently, periodically looking over and smiling. Even his smile sent waves of longing crashing through her. He was just too gorgeous and too wonderful and way, way too considerate. It would be easy to send him on his merry way if he was a jerk or an idiot. But he wasn't. He was personable, witty and interesting, even though the fact that he wasn't willing to talk about his daughter still bothered her.

Alarms went off in her brain, and she wished she had the nerve to ask him about the little girl again. That would certainly cool things off in a hurry. But the question stuck in her throat, so she sat and fought the urge to chew her nails down to the quick and petted Josie instead.

By the time Jared pulled into her driveway, she was a mess. If he left right away, maybe she'd be okay—oh, dear heaven. There was her mom, standing on the porch, her arms crossed in front of her, a small purse hanging on her wrist. How had she forgotten the woman was here?

Erin bit her lip and cringed inwardly.

Jared cut the engine. "Who's that?"

"My mom." She gave him a tight smile. "She's spending the night."

"Oh. Well, I'd like to meet her." He smiled and opened his door.

On the verge of panic, Erin spied her mom walking down the cement walk toward the car. Of course, Wanda James looked perfectly turned-out, as usual, in her blue A-line dress and fake pearls, her ash-blond hair, Clairol Nice 'n Easy 88, gleaming in the sun.

"Great," Erin muttered under her breath, wondering how she was going to deal with Mr. Perfect and the mother from hell at the same time. A girl could only take so much stress.

Resigned to the inevitable, Erin hastily climbed out of the car. "Hey, Mom." She held up a hand.

Her mom smiled tightly, her keen blue gaze on Jared. "And who would this young man be?"

"Mom, this is Jared Warfield…from work," she said, which was pretty much true. "My car broke down, and he drove me home." She looked at Jared. "Jared, this is my mom, Wanda James."

"Nice to meet you." Jared extended his hand.

Her mom warily shook it. "How do you do."

Wanda looked at Erin and held up her purse-encircled wrist. "So, I'm ready to go."

Erin blinked. "Go where?"

Her mom pinched her lips together. "You know. To dinner, like you promised."

Erin stifled a groan. She'd completely forgotten that she'd promised to take her mom to her favorite restaurant for dinner. She looked at her watch. "But, Mom, it's only four-thirty—"

"I like to eat early. Besides, I want to beat the crowds."

"Let's *all* go," Jared said, rubbing his stomach. "I'm starved."

"All right," her mom piped in.

"No!" Erin exclaimed.

He ignored Erin, blast him. "Great, let's go then. This will be my treat," he announced.

Wanda rubbed her arms. "It's cooler than I thought. Let me get my sweater." She turned and went inside.

Worried, Erin glanced at Jared. Why did he want to hang around? And how could he be starved after all of that chicken and jo-joes? "Why do you want to come?"

"Mrs. Sloane and Allison aren't expecting me back yet, and I'm in the mood to go to dinner with you. And your mom seems nice."

Right. Wanda James was a barracuda in a dress, and unfortunately Jared was exactly the kind of guy she would love for Erin to snag—rich and good-looking. Her mom and Brent had shared an eerie rapport and had collectively and on their own put Erin through hell for years.

Erin slanted a glance at Jared. He gave her a reassuring smile. Maybe everything would be all right. He seemed nothing like Brent. He would never jump into cahoots with her mother, would he?

And she really didn't want to come across as petty and mean by refusing to go. Her mom would use that as fuel for more criticism, which Erin certainly didn't need. No, she'd go to dinner and hope she lived through it. How bad could it be?

She snorted under her breath. Jared was, in some stupid corner of her heart, a dream come true, and her mother was a nightmare come to life. Erin was hoping for way too much if she thought she'd come out of this evening with her heart or her self-esteem intact.

But for her own sake she had to try.

A half an hour later, after Jared parked the car in the shade, with the windows cracked for Josie's sake, he sat with Erin and her mom at the rustic wooden table of the casual steak house Erin's mom had chosen.

Boy, had he misjudged the old gal. While she looked like the perfect lady, all the way down to her sensible black pumps, chic but outdated dress, and perfect, blond page-boy, he could tell her good manners were strictly superficial. She never raised her voice and never uttered a harsh word, but she still managed to be critical of every single thing Erin did.

And worst of all, Erin had withered before his eyes and turned into a monosyllabic, spineless waif. She met every criticism and opinion with dull acceptance and never stood up for herself. Where was the woman who had hounded him for an interview and gotten the thing, when he'd been dead set against it?

He looked over at Erin and felt for her. He wondered if she'd ever heard a positive word from her mom.

Wanda's nasal voice brought his attention back around. "Erin, dear, you might want to leave some of that garlic bread—it's full of fat."

Jared looked at Erin, hoping she'd tell her mother to go to hell. But she didn't. She just kept eating the bread, which he guessed was better than nothing.

Her gaze met his, then skittered away. She was clearly miserable. His heart nearly broke. Stubborn, sassy Erin had been reduced to nothing by her mother.

Before he could respond to the distress on her face, Wanda drew his attention away again.

"Jared, did you know Brent, the man Erin let slip away?"

"No?" she responded to his shake of the head. "He was part of the Deville family, as in Deville Automotive."

He sat back and crossed his arms over his chest, disgusted by her blatant mention of Erin's ex-husband and his rich family. Tacky, tacky, tacky.

Wanda continued. "He was such a nice, generous young man." She looked at her daughter. "Erin is going to make some positive changes in her life that will ensure her next marriage lasts. She's realized that she's a little overweight. I might have a weight problem, too, but I watch my fat intake. Yes, Brent was very generous and allowed all of us to live well."

"Yeah," Erin muttered. "Until he took off with his girlfriend and left me broke."

Having apparently not heard Erin, Wanda concluded, "Yes, Erin has a lot to make up for. So, what do you do for a living, Jared?"

Pure outrage came to life in Jared's gut. He wasn't going to sit back and watch Wanda treat Erin like dirt. He had a hunch he was the kind of guy Wanda would love to snag as a son-in-law, one who would allow her to "live well." He wasn't going to sit idly by and watch her talk up her ex-son-in-law at Erin's expense. Luckily, he knew just the thing to put Wanda in her place. And he'd gleefully be the one to do it.

Fastening a bland smile into place, he looked at Wanda, conjuring up an answer to her question. "I don't really do anything for a living. I'm sort of in between jobs right now."

Erin gave a surprised, choked little cough.

"Oh?" Wanda said, her nasal whine coming through like a broken siren. "So you're *unemployed?*" She wrinkled her nose.

He nodded. "Yeah, I guess you could say that. But I do have my recycling route."

"So you own a recycling business?"

He snickered. "Yeah, I *own* it. 'Course, there's not much to own, except my pickup, since I just go around and take newspapers from recycling bins. But I do pretty well. Last week I took in almost a hundred bucks."

Wanda pressed a hand to her chest, looking as though she'd swallowed a fly. "Do you st-steal the papers?"

He winked. "I won't tell if you don't."

The waiter brought their food. Erin took a huge gulp of water. Her curious gaze met his over her glass, clearly asking, What are you doing? But he shrugged and smiled. He could just tell Wanda off, but figured scaring her spitless as a possible son-in-law from hell would make a bigger impression.

"Let's dig in," he said heartily, then looked at Wanda's plate. "Oh, man, they gave you the thicker steak. Mine's sorta thin, and probably a little overdone." He picked up her steak with his fingers. "I'll trade. Seein' as how you're watching your fat, you won't mind, now, will you, dear?" He plopped the thick piece of meat onto his plate, then picked his up and tossed it onto Wanda's plate. "There you go. Thanks a bunch, babe."

Wanda, being the "lady" she was, pressed her lips together and simply stared at him.

He heard choking sounds from Erin's direction, but concentrated on shoving his napkin in his collar, like a bib. That done, he looked up and saw Wanda dubiously eyeing his getup. He shrugged and picked up his knife and fork. "I'm serious when it comes to food." He proceeded to cut his steak.

Wanda sat stiffly, her mouth puckered like a prune, shaking her head. Jared glanced at Erin, who had managed to corral her laughter to eat her meal. At least she didn't look so darn sad and woeful. But his job wasn't half-done. He figured he had years of put-downs to make up for, and while he realized nothing could take away the pain of having a witch for a mother, he could at least do this small thing to put Wanda in her place and show support for Erin.

Support he owed her for kissing her when nothing could come of it.

Except for some mild food shoveling and gulping, he minded his manners for a while, just long enough to lure Wanda into a false sense of security.

As they ate, Wanda daintily cut her steak. "Tell me about your family, Jared."

He stopped midchew, swallowed hard, then grabbed a hunk of napkin and wiped his mouth. "I don't get to see my dad much, seeing as how I like to sleep in, and visiting hours at the pen are in the morning. But I manage to get down to Salem once in a while to visit. It's nice, since I can swing by the mental hospital on the way down and visit my brother, too." He tapped his head. "Hasn't been right since the overdose. And my mom, well, she's doin' great. Her worm farm is goin' gangbusters—"

"Worm farm?" Wanda asked, her eyes the size of Oreos.

"Hell, yeah, the biggest in Oregon. She's raking the dough in with that little enterprise. Why, she must make ten, eleven grand a year. She's got herself a nice mobile home and a great husband. 'Course, Marv isn't home a lot, cause of his problems with the IRS, but she's happy enough. I park my Winnebago right next door and she watches the kids all the time."

Wanda's brows almost disappeared into her hairline. "Kids?"

He nodded and smiled proudly. "Sure, sure. Got six of 'em. 'Course with Cody staying at juvey and Janie on the run there's only four now, but that'll change soon enough, with Maria expectin' and all."

"Maria?"

"Now, now, don't you worry. I'm not married. I've agreed to do my duty and provide child support. I'm not one to ignore my responsibilities. I've done right by Jason and Jeremy all along."

The look of pure horror on Wanda's face was perfect.

He winked at Erin, who had covered her mouth with her hand, and dug back into his food. He should have considered a career on the stage.

Finally Erin laughed out loud. Next to Allison's cute little belly laugh, it was the best thing he'd ever heard.

The ride home from the restaurant passed in total silence. Erin sat next to Jared, trying not to explode with pent-up laughter. The look on her mother's face during his "act" had been priceless. It was the only time in recent memory that Wanda had ever been totally, wonderfully speechless.

There was no doubt in Erin's mind that Jared had concocted his little story to put her mom in her place. Erin supposed she should be mad; what he'd done could be construed as unkind. But her mom had been unkind to Erin for her whole life. A little payback seemed harmless. Besides, Wanda James possessed a will of steel and a stubborn streak as wide as the Willamette River. Jared's little show wasn't going to bother her for long.

While his scheme had been underhanded, Erin would cherish his intentions because he'd done it for her, to show his support. No one had ever cared enough about her to do something so outlandishly devilish.

Her heart turned over in her chest, warming her from the inside out.

Score one very huge point for Jared.

As soon as he pulled into Erin's driveway and stopped, her mom jumped out of his BMW, which was a dead giveaway that his life story was more than likely fake, and hurried to the house.

Erin shot Jared a wry grin. "She probably thinks that your jailbird father is going to spring from the trunk, ax in hand, and kill her."

He shook his head apologetically. "Man, I'm so sorry. I don't know what came over me. I just—"

"No, don't be." She held up a hand. "Trust me, she deserved it."

"Maybe, but I'm not usually that inconsiderate." His jaw flexed. "She made me so damn mad, sitting there, putting you down like that. Why did you let her get away with it?"

She shifted uneasily. Despite her best intentions, she *had* rolled over and let her mom beat her down. "Old habit, I guess."

"Yeah, well maybe it's a habit you should break."

Well, duh. Of course he was right. But heavens, the thought of standing up to her mom, who had always been able to cut Erin down with a few derisive words, scared her to death, even though her mom had shown small signs of softening lately.

He spoke again. "And I have to tell you, I admire the hell out of you for not killing your mom or going nuts. She's a lot to put up with, isn't she?"

She turned and stared at him, stunned and pleased by his supportive statement, so different from Brent's "why can't you just get along with your mother" attitude. "Yes, she is." She smiled. "And I'll think about what you said—" She broke off when she saw her mom open the front door and give her the evil eye.

Erin crossed her arms over her chest. "No way am I going in there," she said, determined to take a small stand, right here, right now.

"Good for you." Jared's pager sounded, shrill in the confined space of his car. "Hold on." He glanced at the pager and turned it off. "Can I go inside and use your phone?"

She wanted to scream, Heck, no! They'd pressed their luck with her mom already. But Erin was determined to be gracious, so she cleared her throat and said, "Uh, sure, no problem."

She snatched up her purse. But she'd grabbed the wrong end, and everything in the leather satchel dumped out onto the floor of his car. Muttering dark thoughts under her breath about how Jared would now think she was a klutz as well as a doormat, she got out of the car, turned and scooped everything up. She shoved it all back inside the purse, waved to Josie and slammed the car door.

Jared followed her to the porch. She opened the front door and stepped inside. "The phone's in the kitchen," she said, waving a hand in the general direction of where he should go, hoping her mom wasn't in there.

He stepped around Erin, his big body reminding her

what his lips felt like on hers and how much her own body stupidly wanted more. "Thanks," he said.

Erin looked down the hall and was relieved when she saw her mom close the door to the guest room. Glad that Wanda was out of their hair for the moment, Erin gnawed on her thumbnail, her heart fluttering. Why did Jared always manage to fluster her like this?

She rolled her eyes and threw her bag down. Get over it. She'd give him his privacy for his phone call, and then he'd leave and she'd be fine. Her blood would cool, and she'd forget how much she liked everything about him and how good it had felt when he'd stood up for her. Because of the gaping wound Brent had sliced in her heart, that was the way it had to be.

She heard Jared's deep voice from the kitchen, then specifically heard a swearword. She stepped toward the kitchen door, then heard the phone slam down in its cradle. She froze, puzzled.

Jared stormed out of the kitchen, grim-faced. "I gotta go."

Had he been planning on staying? Ignoring that disturbing question, she focused on the concern rippling through her. "What's wrong?" Had something happened to his daughter?

He shook his head and opened the screen door. "Just a family emerg—uh, situation." He strode across the porch. "Be sure to call a tow truck. If you need a car to use while yours is being fixed, I have a company van I can lend you for a few days."

Erin stopped at the door and held the screen open, wishing he trusted her enough to confide in her about his little girl. "No, that's all right. I'll get a loaner or something." She had to sever any ties between them, no matter how small.

He paused. "You're one stubborn woman, you know that? It wouldn't kill you to accept a favor from me."

She shook her head. "I appreciate the thought, but no. I'll manage." He was too tempting, and she wasn't about to tempt herself straight back into heartbreak hell.

Regret, or something that looked like it, swept briefly across his face, but it was gone instantly.

She probably imagined it.

"Okay. Thanks for the company." He held up a hand, then moved toward his car.

She halfheartedly waved back. Leaning her cheek against the cool doorjamb, she watched him back out of her driveway and speed away.

She turned and went inside, wishing things were different. If only she could rewind her life, back to before Brent's shabby treatment had heaped itself on top of the wound her father's death had caused, adding to her emotional scars. There was a time when she believed in true love and soul mates and that kind of romantic nonsense. She'd trusted Brent, and thought he was her one true love. But he'd hurt her in the worst way possible, deep in her heart, and that was something she would never forget. Or let happen again.

No, she wouldn't let herself care for any man ever again. Not even a wonderful, supportive, melt-her-into-a-puddle man like Jared.

Chapter Six

The automatic double doors opened with a *whoosh*. Jared walked through, dread turning his blood cold, and hesitated as the antiseptic hospital smell hit him full force. He nearly gagged. He'd never be able to step into a hospital without remembering the time he'd spent by his father's bedside, watching him die, or the agonizing hours he'd spent in the emergency room, praying with everything in him that Carolyn would live despite her mortal injuries. The smell, the colors, the hushed voices. It all held nothing but bad, painful memories of a dying man, his confused, tortured son and the wounded woman both men had failed.

He ruthlessly shoved the memories back deep down inside. Allison needed him now, and nothing—not even the searing pain he felt thinking about his father and Carolyn—would keep him from her side.

Jared followed the signs to the emergency room, praying Allison was all right. Mrs. Sloane had told him on the phone that Allison had fallen and cut open her head. Supposedly she was going to be fine, but he had to see for himself and hold her in his arms before he could allow himself to relax. Allison was everything to him, and the one person he was certain would love him unconditionally. He couldn't bear the thought of anything happening to her.

And damn if he shouldn't have been home with his little angel instead of wasting his time on some dumb date and hanging out with Erin.

With practiced ease he let the deserved guilt flow over him. He hadn't managed to save Carolyn when she'd needed him the most. He'd been too focused on escaping his own torment by building up his business to pay enough attention to his little sister, the wounded soul who'd escaped the pain of their dysfunctional family and their notoriety by running with a crowd of drug and alcohol abusers. She'd paid for her bad judgment and his inexcusable lack of interest when the motorcycle she'd been riding on had missed a curve and crashed into a tree, killing both her and her creepy, drunk boyfriend, who was Allison's father.

I'm so sorry, Care-Bear.

Yeah, he'd failed Carolyn, big-time, but he wouldn't fail her daughter by becoming involved with a reporter who could ruin Allison's innocent life.

After a terse conversation with a harried-looking nurse at the front desk, he stepped through a door and moved to exam room five, where he'd been told Allison and Mrs. Sloane waited.

He stepped into the room and his blood froze. Allison sat sucking her thumb on Mrs. Sloane's generous lap. A narrow bandage had been wrapped around Allison's blond, curl-topped head and he could distinctly see the tracks of her tears on her chubby, pale cheeks.

He closed his eyes and took a deep breath. He needed to stay calm and cool-headed, even though the sight of his little girl with a damn bandage on her head drove all rational thought from his mind.

Mrs. Sloane, her round face as pale as snow, looked up. "Mr. Warfield," she said, her gray eyes glassy with tears.

Allison lifted her head. "Dada!" she cried, struggling to get off Mrs. Sloane's lap. "Dada!"

He walked toward them, his arms outstretched. "Ally-Bear." A second later his precious darling was in his arms, snuggled against him, her little-girl scent surrounding him.

He held her tight, thanking God that she was all right, vowing to protect her no matter what.

Allison pulled away and looked up at him, her big blue eyes wide. "Owee." She pressed a chubby hand to her head. "Owee, Dada."

He buried his face in her curls, then pressed a gentle kiss to the top of her head. "I know, Ally-Bear, I know."

Mrs. Sloane wrung her hands but remained silent.

He pressed his lips together and looked at the nanny. "What happened?"

"She stumbled and fell against the coffee table in the family room."

He looked at Allison's head. "How many stitches?"

"Five."

He clenched his jaw.

Mrs. Sloane pulled off her glasses and wiped her red-rimmed eyes. "I'm so sorry, Mr. Warfield. I was right there, but she tripped over a toy—"

He held up a hand and cut her off. "This isn't your fault. All children fall down." *And I should have been there.*

"I know," Mrs. Sloane said, running a hand through her disheveled gray hair. She looked exhausted. "But even so…"

"Why don't you go on home." He adjusted Allison in

his arms. She pressed her face into the side of his neck. "I'll stay here with Allison."

"Oh, no, I couldn't leave—"

"You need to rest, and there's no reason for both of us to stay. They said they wanted to hold her for observation?"

"Yes, since it's so late and she lost consciousness for a brief time."

He squeezed Allison tighter against him. The thought of losing her cut across his soul, reminding him of how important it was to keep her safe.

How important it was to stay away from Erin James.

He finally convinced Mrs. Sloane to go home. After a long conversation with the emergency room physician, who assured Jared that Allison was fine and that they were simply keeping her for observation as a precautionary measure, Allison was moved to a private room on the pediatric floor.

They settled in and a nurse delivered a late dinner for Allison. Jared sat in the room's lone chair, Allison snuggled into his arms, and he coaxed a sleepy little angel to eat the macaroni and cheese and take a few sips of apple juice by pretending the spoon and tippy-cup were a choo-choo train. She ate a few bites, but refused any more, saying it didn't taste like the "cheesy pasta" he routinely made.

After several renditions of his customized version of the Itsy-Bitsy Ally, complete with hand motions and silly voices, she fell asleep nestled against his heart, her breathing even and strong.

He sat for a long time, simply holding her in his arms, watching her sleep, a fierce, primal sense of protection moving through him. The doctor had said she was going to be fine, as good as new. Even so, Jared fought the feeling of helplessness pouring through him. He hated seeing Allison this way, hated the feeling of absolute panic that rushed through him when he thought about failing her like he'd failed Carolyn.

Darkness fell and shrouded the room. Inevitably, painful memories sliced through him. A year fell away, and the most terrible day of his life ripped through his brain like a razor-sharp dagger. The E.R. waiting room. His constant, desperate prayers. The doctor's somber expression. Carolyn was dead.

My fault.

Suddenly, in the blink of an eye he was sixteen again, sitting in another hospital room, holding another hand. His father. Dying. Withering away. Alone and unhappy.

Women had drifted in and out of his father's life, always more interested in his millions than in him. He'd married a few of those women, including Jared's mother and Carolyn's mother, but none had stayed. They all took the old bird's money but never tried to love the man who hid his pain and loneliness behind a wall of icy indifference that extended even to his son.

But Jared had stayed until the end, desperately hoping to discover a tiny grain of heart in his father. But he'd found nothing but the familiar hurt and disappointment. No words of love had ever passed from his father's lips. The old man had died as frigid and alone as he'd lived. All of the women who'd professed to love him and married him were long gone—and rich.

Jared had sworn then and there that he wouldn't relive the old man's misery by letting a woman close, only to take advantage and leave him alone.

That kind of love carried a terrible price he wasn't willing to pay.

He shifted Allison in his arms, trying to ease the stiffness from his body. Ever so gently he stood and moved closer to the crib and placed her in it. She whimpered once, but he cooed nonsense words to her and rubbed her back and she settled back into sleep.

He needed to move around, maybe get some coffee to stay awake. He stepped out into the hallway and jammed on the brakes.

Erin. Dressed in ragged jeans and a gray sweatshirt, hovering at the end of the corridor, her bottom lip held between her teeth. Surprise ripped through him, then anger. How dare she bring her little reporter butt down here to intrude on his private life?

He clenched his hands into fists and stalked closer. ''Don't you have any sense of decency? Why are you here, sniffing around?''

She shook her head and held up her hands. ''I left my tape recorder in your car, and I need it back.'' She looked at him as if he'd grown horns. ''That's all, I swear.''

Jared stopped and regarded her warily. Maybe she wasn't out for blood. ''Your tape recorder?''

She nodded.

He took her elbow and firmly led her away from Allison's room. ''How did you find me?''

She looked sheepish. ''I...uh, sort of conned it out of your secretary.''

He put his fists on his hips and narrowed his eyes. ''Again?''

''I had to. The rest of 'The Bachelor Chronicles' is due tomorrow, and I can't complete it without my recorder. I accidentally dumped my bag in your car and left the recorder....''

He sighed, then rubbed the bridge of his nose. ''Fine,'' he intoned, digging in his pocket. ''Here are the keys.''

Erin looked at him and cocked her head to the side. "Are you all right? You look like h—uh, terrible."

He palmed the keys. "Gee, thanks."

She took a few tentative steps nearer, her face pressed into a half-concerned, half-speculative expression. "Is this your 'family situation?' What happened?"

He clenched his jaw and held up a rigid hand, forcing himself to remember what Erin was—a reporter. "I don't want to talk about it."

She stiffly inclined her head. "Fair enough. But it's late. Shouldn't you go home and get some rest?"

Her light scent washed over him, which, along with her prying, bothered him. "Why are you asking me all of these questions? The interview's over."

She frowned and shoved her hands in the pockets of her jeans. "Look, I only meant that…no, no, you're right. The interview *is* over." She turned away, then looked back, her mouth pressed into a thin line.

He was being a first-class jerk. "Erin, I'm sorry. It's been a terrible night."

She raised a brow. "I…I didn't mean to make you mad."

"I know."

She put her hand on his arm and he almost flinched. "I'm guessing visiting hours are almost over," she said.

He nodded wearily, ignoring how much he liked it when she touched him, how much he wanted to take her in his arms and unload his problems. Man, oh, man, what was wrong with him?

"Then why stay? You can come back first thing in the morning." She paused. "Besides, I could use a ride to my friend Colleen's house to pick up her car. I wasn't sure how long it would take me to find you, so I didn't have the cab wait."

He couldn't leave Allison here alone. No way. He needed to be the first person she saw when she woke up. "I can't leave. I'll walk you out to the garage and get your recorder and then we'll call another cab. But do me a favor. No questions."

"Whatever you say," she replied with a wave. "I just need my recorder and a way to Colleen's house."

They walked to the parking garage in silence. He unlocked his car and she retrieved her recorder from under the passenger seat, then they started back toward the hospital.

"I guess I owe you an apology for jumping all over you back there," he said, breaking the uncomfortable silence. "I thought you'd come looking for a story."

She looked at him. "A story? Why would you think that?"

He lifted a shoulder, remembering his fears about keeping Allison protected from the media. "You're a reporter, remember?"

She nodded. "Yeah, okay, I guess I can see why, even though you and I finished our interview. Besides, I usually do human-interest stuff, not news. At least not yet. I'm sort of looking for my big break, you know, a good juicy story that would convince my editor I can do harder stuff."

Harder stuff. Like maybe how a wealthy local man had adopted his dead sister's daughter, who happened to be the granddaughter of a big-time Hollywood star, and that the man had been too busy to be with his daughter and keep her safe? He felt guilty for even being with Erin.

They stepped into the elevator, and her sweet, rose-tinged scent washed over him. Without warning, his mind switched gears, and memories of their picnic and dinner popped into his mind. Her smiles had melted his heart, and laughing with her had brought about a warm contentment he'd never experienced with a woman before. And her kisses. Man, she'd tasted and felt better than anything…

Damn. He didn't need this right now. He needed to concentrate on Allison, not on some rose-scented reporter who could do a hatchet job on his family. Erin had already dug around and found out about Allison. He should just walk away, even though he wanted to pull Erin close and kiss her again.

His body didn't seem to get that. By the time the elevator stopped on the pediatric floor, his earlier lethargy had disappeared, leaving hard-edged, impatient desire in its wake. After the crummy night he'd had, he wanted the distraction of Erin in his arms.

Don't be a fool, buddy.

They stepped out of the elevator. He fought his desire, scrambling for reason and sanity. Erin James was the last thing he, or Allison, needed, for so many reasons. Taking a deep breath, he urged himself to calm down and forget how much he wanted to pull Erin into his arms.

"Jared?" She stopped and leaned closer. "Are you all right?"

He swallowed. "I'm fine."

She put her hand on his arm. "Are you sure? Do you want to talk about what's going on?"

So she wanted to talk. He clenched his jaw, trying to ignore the hole her hand was burning on his arm and focus on the disappointment and anger growing in him. She *was* out for a story. "It's none of your business."

"I know." She leaned forward and looked at his face. "But you seem upset. I thought I could help."

He kept his eyes off her to hold on to his tenuous control. "Help?" He wanted to laugh. All she could help with was the red-hot desire racing through him. "How could you help?"

She skimmed her hand up his arm to his shoulder. "Sometimes it helps to talk about things."

Unable to resist, he looked at her pale hand on him, wishing she would slide it farther down, into his shirt, over his chest....

With a muttered oath he forced his gaze away. Yeah, sure she wanted to talk. And work him for some information on why he was here. Damn her for lying to him and for trying to use him. Why not kiss her when she had no qualms about using him to get a story?

One kiss meant nothing. His resolve to resist her burned away like dry kindling in a hot fire, fueled by the anger smoldering in his belly. He looked around the deserted hall, and in one smooth motion he stepped into an alcove, grabbed her hand and pulled her close until her face was an inch from his. "I don't need your help with anything but this."

And then he kissed her, long and slow and hot, his tongue moving smoothly, slickly into her warm, sweet mouth.

She pressed herself to him, returning his kiss fully. She was warm and soft in his arms, something real and wonderful that, surprisingly, made his relentless anxiety about Allison temporarily fade away until it was an indistinct lump in a far corner of his brain.

He tried to hold on to his anger and remember why he was doing this. Disappointment. Using him. Using her. But all that faded in a flash, and he hazily let it go. Nothing mattered but how right she felt in his arms and how he wanted her so bad he couldn't think straight.

He pulled her closer, needing to lose himself in the wonderful way she made him feel.

But she pressed on his chest and pulled away. "Jared. Stop, please."

Stop.

He jerked away, reason crashing down on him. What was he thinking, kissing a reporter within feet of Allison's hospital room? He had no business getting involved with Erin on any level. Because of Allison he had no intention of seeing Erin again.

And, obviously, they were on the same page. She'd told him to stop, and he would. He had to. Even if Allison weren't involved, he'd make himself walk away. He didn't want any woman getting under his skin only to use him and leave.

He looked at Erin. She'd pressed a visibly shaking hand to her mouth. She stared at him with wide, stunned, dark-green eyes, and he had the insane desire to pull her back into his arms and lose himself in her scent. He yanked on his watch. "I'm sorry," he said. "I shouldn't have done that. This ends here, all right?"

She nodded. "The article's done, so…well, I won't need to interview you anymore."

"Right." He tried to ignore the strange shaft of disappointment that shot through him when he thought about never seeing her again.

She paused and gave him a thoughtful look. "And just so you can rest easy, I think of you as a friend now, and I'm not out for any kind of story about your…anything in your life, okay?"

He nodded, amazed at her perceptiveness and relieved by her statement. "Okay. Thanks."

"Bye." And then, with a sad little smile, she turned and walked away.

He wanted to call her back, craving her company. But he didn't. As much as he might like to see Erin again, this was really the best thing that could have happened.

Even though his foolish heart seemed to have other ideas.

Chapter Seven

Erin stayed up most of the night and somehow managed to pound out the rest of "The Bachelor Chronicles." Despite Jared and Hilary's disastrous, failed date, Erin had racked her brain and scraped together enough details for a decent story, judiciously leaving out how Hilary had stomped off, a muddy paw print on her rear end.

All night Erin had alternately relived her and Jared's sizzling kiss and lingered on warm thoughts of Jared—had he really concocted that silly story just for her?—even though his refusal to talk about his daughter should knock some darn sense into her. Erin was sure he'd been at the hospital because of his daughter, but he obviously didn't trust her enough to confide in her.

Ouch.

Didn't matter. Her work was done and she wouldn't be seeing Jared again. Ever.

When she arrived at work, having left early enough to avoid her mom's inevitable rant about acceptable boyfriend material, she dumped her briefcase on her desk, sternly telling herself that she was glad she was finished with the assignment that had nearly turned her, and her emotions, inside out. She would finally be able to put some much-needed distance between her and Jared and get on with her life. A lonely life, yes, but safe from the painful kind of damage Brent had inflicted.

"Erin!" Joe's voice boomed across the room from his office doorway. "Get in here."

Erin dug the last section of "The Bachelor Chronicles" out of her briefcase and followed her boss into his office.

She handed him the copy. "Here you go. It's done."

Joe tossed the papers down onto his desk. "I'll read it later. I've got bigger things to talk about right now." He gestured to the chair next to Erin. "Sit."

Erin complied, puzzled by Joe's dismissal of "The Bachelor Chronicles," his latest obsession. "What's up?"

"Do you know Jared Warfield has a daughter?"

"Uh, yeah, why?"

"Because we've just received an anonymous tip that Jared's daughter is in the hospital because the nanny was negligent."

Oh, no. Her suspicions confirmed. That explained Jared's edginess and the simmering anger she'd thought was perhaps directed at her—until they'd kissed.

"Really?" She attempted to keep her voice casual, as though she hadn't seen Jared at that very hospital last night, as though she'd hadn't known for three weeks that Jared had a daughter. Joe would wonder, loudly, why she hadn't pounced on the story last night, and she really didn't have a good excuse. She'd been curious, but her journalistic drive had sputtered to a halt when she'd seen how worn-out he'd looked.

She'd been thinking of Jared, not her job.

And now, Jared's reaction when she'd shown up at the

hospital last night made sense. He assumed she was there to jump on his misfortune for her own gain. Funny how that thought hurt.

Joe nodded. "Yup, really. Do you know who the kid's grandmother was?"

"Some former actress named Janet Worthington?"

Joe loosened his stained tie and nodded. "Apparently Jared adopted his sister's kid after his sister was killed in a motorcycle crash. It was big news because of the kid's grandmother, and of course because of the Warfield name and her brother's business. It was front-page stuff, but before anything was printed, Warfield hushed it all up and almost put one reporter in the hospital, and the furor died down. But now the kid's in the hospital and we can be the first one on the story."

Erin's heart sank like a rock and her stomach twisted. This conversation was going to a place she absolutely, positively did not want to go.

"Get over to Good Samaritan Hospital and get the details. You know Warfield, which should be to our advantage, right? Use that edge, that inside track. We can scoop this up now before anyone else."

Problem was, she didn't want to get the scoop on Jared. She'd promised him she wouldn't go after any stories about anything connected to him, and she'd meant it. This would hurt him and maybe his daughter, too. No kid deserved that.

She chewed on a thumbnail. "Joe, I don't think I can—"

"What do you mean?" he blustered. "You've been hot to do bigger news, and here's your chance. This could be your big break, Erin. Don't mess it up."

Oh, no. She couldn't do this. Even though she'd been after something that would get her out of rinky-dink human-interest stories and into hard journalism, or as hard as it got at the *Beacon,* she couldn't go after this story.

Jared's angry reaction last night was just a preview of what she'd get if she bothered him this morning, her tape recorder in hand, breaking her promise.

Oh, yes, by the way. Tell me more about your adopted daughter and her dead mother and your negligent nanny so I can put it in the newspaper.

Her stomach tightened painfully. Jared would crucify her for something that sleazy. Sure, she was a reporter and had to set aside personal conflict. But deep down, hounding Jared did bother her. He deserved privacy, especially now, with his daughter in the hospital.

But then again she had a job to do. A job she loved and could call her own, a job she needed. She had to shove her personal feelings aside and forget about how much it bothered her to intrude on Jared's family crisis.

Maybe she could convince Jared it was better for her to write the story. A small bubble of hope expanded in her. She could soften the edges, tell his side of things. Maybe he would go for that.

Probably not.

"Well?" Joe insisted. "I don't have all day."

She rose, sighing, then pressed a hand to her roiling stomach. "Okay, okay. I'll go right over." A hard lump of apprehension rose in her chest. "But I can tell you right now, Warfield isn't going to like this, Joe."

He waved a hand in the air. "Too bad. No one likes their personal business printed. Just get the dirt."

The dirt. That sounded pretty ugly. But ugly or not, this was her chance at a promotion. Her self-respect as a reporter was at stake. She had to find a way to make this work.

And, boy, did she have an agonizing choice to make. Do her job well or protect the man who had touched her heart and soul.

A light knock sounded on Allison's hospital door.

Jared stood and wearily stretched the kinks from his body, then went to the door and cautiously pulled it open.

To his surprise, Erin stood on the other side, her lip tugged between her teeth, looking really, really good in a short-sleeved, clingy white sweater and dark-blue jeans that hugged her curves perfectly. She had her fiery hair twisted up into some kind of bun thingy on the back of her head, and several curls had escaped from the bun to frame her face.

Red flags flapped around in his brain. "Are you here as a friend or as a reporter?"

Hurt rose in her eyes. She backed away, blinking.

Contrition burned inside of him. Erin had assured him last night that she wouldn't pursue any stories about his family, and he believed her.

It wouldn't hurt to talk to her, but not in Allison's room. "Hey, I'm sorry," he whispered, stepping into the hall. "It's just that every time I've been in a hospital, reporters circle, looking for action."

Her face relaxed and she gazed up at him, her leaf-green eyes wide and concerned. "How are you?"

He kept his gaze steady on her, wondering how much he should tell her. Even though the doctor had reassured him again this morning that Allison was going to be fine, the stress of spending the night in her room, listening for her to call out to him while he was haunted by memories of other fateful hospital stays, had taken their toll. He felt exhausted and keyed-up all at once and in desperate need of a sympathetic ear. Hospitals always stressed him out.

He rubbed his neck, wishing he could take a long, hot shower. "I'm okay."

She touched his arm with her slender, warm hand. "You don't look okay."

He sucked in a deep breath, wanting to cover Erin's hand with his and absorb her warmth into himself. Should he confide in her? Once again, he looked into her soft-green eyes, looking for an ulterior motive. But she simply stared back at him, her eyes completely free of guile, and his instincts, which were usually right on, told him he could believe what she'd said last night about not pursuing any stories concerning him or his family. "Actually, I'm not. Allison—"

A janitor mopping the hallway broke in. "Don't mind me. I'll just mop around you."

Jared waved his hand in the air. "Fine." He turned back to Erin. "Anyway, my daughter fell and hit her head."

She raised a delicate brow and cocked a corner of her lush mouth. "Ah, so you've finally decided to confide in me about your daughter."

He stared at her, then tilted his head to the side and returned her smile. "I guess so."

"Why?"

He lifted a shoulder. "You've obviously known about Allison for weeks and you haven't jumped on the knowledge in order to get a story. You've proven that I can trust you."

A shadow moved across her face, but it came and went so quickly that he was sure he imagined it.

"Go on," she said.

"So, you know that I adopted her when my sister died last year." Pain and familiar guilt knifed through his heart, but he continued despite the ache. "She ran with a bad crowd, and she and Allison's father were killed when he crashed his motorcycle into a tree. Thank God Allison was staying with me when it happened.''

"I'm so sorry, Jared.''

His gaze moved to the door of Allison's room and he forced himself to think of the darling little girl sleeping in the crib inside and of how much joy she'd brought into his life. "Allison's going to be fine, but hospitals…well.'' He shook his head. "I hate them.''

"Most people dislike hospitals,'' Erin said.

"This is more than dislike. I've never walked away from a hospital without planning a funeral. Add that to the stress of waiting for the press to descend.''

"Why do you assume that will happen?''

He laughed humorlessly. "It's the drill. I'm a Warfield. My dad was a well-known businessman, Carolyn's mom, Allison's grandmother, was famous. Carolyn's wild lifestyle attracted the press in droves.'' He looked up and down the hallway. "Actually, I'm surprised some reporter hasn't shown up, looking to make a story out of my little girl falling down. Was the nanny at fault? How about the dad?'' He snorted under his breath. "It's disgusting.''

A pained look crossed Erin's face. She shook her head, mumbled something under her breath, and blew out a fat puff of air. "Jared, I have to come clean.'' She held up her hand and revealed a small tape recorder. "I *did* come here for a story.''

Angry fire flashed through him. "What the hell?'' he ground out. He yanked her hand out and the recorder clattered to the floor. "I trusted you.''

"Jared, relax. It's not turned on, I swear.''

He narrowed his eyes and flung her hand away. "How did you know my daughter was here?'' he snapped. "I bet you poked around last night and figured out what was going on, right?''

She glanced at the floor. "No. We got an anonymous tip at the paper this morning. My editor called me in and told me to follow up on the story."

He shook his head. Why had he let his guard down and trusted her when so much was at stake? "Give me a break. And I suppose you thought since we…kissed last night you could sashay in here and I'd fill you in on the details between kisses." He snorted derisively. "You're nothing but a rabid reporter out for dirt."

Her face twisted and she swung around, her hands clenched at her sides. "Look, I didn't tape anything, all right?" She picked the recorder up and popped the tape from the machine and handed it to him. "I came clean on my own."

Surprised, he took the tape. "Why didn't you record anything?"

She shrugged, then looked at him, honesty and integrity shining from her large eyes. "You were talking to me like a…friend, and I don't rat out friends," she softly said. "I told you last night I wouldn't go after any stories, and even though my boss badgered me into coming down here, I realize now that I meant what I said. I swear. I don't want to hurt you or your daughter."

He let out a rough breath, then rubbed the back of his neck, torn between wanting to believe her and wanting to fall back on old, safe habits and shut her out. He paced across the hall, looking at the ceiling, wondering if he could really trust Erin. She hadn't used her knowledge of Allison, she'd told him the truth on her own and had readily surrendered the tape. And she hadn't personally given him any reason to doubt her word.

He finally turned back to her. He smiled ruefully. "I'm sorry I came down on you."

She let out an audible sigh and her face relaxed. "You

can trust me. Everything you told me is off the record."
She moved toward him and put her hand on his arm.
"Okay?"

Warm sparks raced up his arm. He pressed his hand over
hers, liking the feel of her slender hand under his.
"Okay." He leaned over and kissed her mouth lightly,
then pulled her into his arms, letting her rose scent and
soft, welcoming curves soothe his weary senses. "Off the
record."

She put her arms around his waist and nestled close. His
chest tightened, spreading warmth throughout his body,
and it felt damn good to be able to trust her.

His doubts about her and his edginess faded away, and
all he could think about was how much he liked her. She'd
proven her loyalty, proven that she wouldn't betray him.

He didn't want to let her go yet.

"Hey," he said, pulling away and looking down into
her face. "I'm taking Allison home shortly. Wanna
come?"

She blinked. After a moment's hesitation, a brilliant
smile appeared on her face. "Okay."

He pressed a light kiss to her mouth. "Great. I have one
last meeting with Allison's doctor, and then I have to
check her out. I don't want you to have to wait, so I'll
give you directions and I'll meet you at my house, all
right?"

She nodded. "Sounds good to me."

Sounded pretty good to him, too.

Erin slipped back into work without letting Joe see her.
She needed to make sure that Colleen's man of the hour
was still picking her up from work so Erin could still use
her car.

Colleen confirmed that detail, and after Erin gathered

her things, she followed Jared's directions and drove to his house, apprehension running rampant inside of her. Was she a fool to ignore her common sense and follow her stupid dreams and meet him here?

She shrugged off her worries, determined to live for the moment—just this once.

To her surprise his home was situated down a long gravel road far off the beaten path, surrounded by pine trees and lush vegetation. When she rounded a bend in the road and the house came into view, she could only stare.

The place was a veritable mansion, right out of a fairy tale.

Made entirely of deep-red brick, the huge, rambling two-story residence rose majestically in front of her like a castle. The sun gleamed off the many mullioned windows that marched across the front of the house. Lush, green ivy crept up the sides of the house like velvet. A turret, complete with stained-glass windows, dominated one end of the building.

A huge front porch ran the entire length of the two-story home. Dark mission-style furniture sat clustered near the front door, and a porch swing dominated the end of the porch. Flowerpots decorated the front of the porch, and numerous window boxes, filled with trailing, colorful plants and flowers, hung on the wood railing.

What looked like acres of perfectly manicured emerald green lawn rolled out from the base of the porch steps like lush carpet. Jared had obviously put his gardening skills to work; flowers and shrubs and huge trees bloomed in profusion around the gigantic yard, adding color and texture to the setting. She even spotted a bubbling fountain, complete with a statue, in a far corner of the huge yard.

The house and grounds were gorgeous and beautifully done and a place fit for a king.

Oh, my.

She spied Jared's car parked in front of the attached, four-car garage. He'd beaten her here. She pulled up next to his vehicle and turned off her car's ignition.

Jared appeared in the front door, a still-bandaged Allison in his arms.

Erin's heart gave a little jerk.

He crossed the porch and descended the stairs. "So, what do you think?"

"I think," she said with a wry smile, "that it's beautiful."

She rose from the car and looked around the front of the house and saw a tiny doll carriage sitting on the porch. And in the far corner of the yard by the fountain sat another brightly colored toy.

Allison's toys.

Her heart warmed.

She looked at Allison, who waved and gurgled, "Hi!"

"Hi." Erin waved back and grinned. "I'm Erin."

"Hair-win." Allison beamed.

Jared smiled and nuzzled Allison's cheek. "That's right, Ally-Bear. Hair-win."

Just as Erin's heart was about to melt like warm candy in her chest, two dogs burst from the front door and bounded down the porch stairs. Erin immediately recognized Josie, and realized a second later that the other mutt was the dog who'd been singing in the car with Jared the first day she'd met him.

Both dogs yipped as they danced around Jared's legs, demanding attention.

Allison pointed to Josie. "Do-sie." Then she pointed to the other dog. "Fwed." She clapped her hands together and laughed in glee when both dogs stood on their hind legs and pawed the air with their paws.

"Hi!" Allison waved her tiny, plump hand at the dogs.

Jared squatted down, Allison still in his arms, and gave each dog its share of attention. Allison clung to him, peppering tiny kisses on his jaw. A lock of her hair was tangled in Jared's ear. Josie's paws were on his knees and Fred's nose was buried in his side pocket. Erin met his contented gaze, and she was stunned and touched by the total happiness and satisfaction shining from the cappuccino-colored depths of his eyes.

A strong desire to squat down next to Jared and join that perfect little picture came over Erin, but she held back, feeling the outsider in all of the kissing and excitement. They were a family. The sort of family she never had but always wanted.

I'll never be a part of this, she thought.

Her heart split wide open in her chest, and at that very moment she realized she had only scratched the surface of the kind of man Jared was. Worse, she wanted to know more.

Much more.

Everything.

He was proving himself to be a down-to-earth, gentle, hardworking man with a strong sense of familial devotion and loyalty. And he'd stood up for her. He was so much more than the hot bachelor she'd met almost a month ago at Warfield's. And he was so much harder to resist.

As she followed Jared, Allison and the dogs into the house, she wondered what she'd gotten herself into.

And how in the world she was going to get herself out.

"Bye-bye, Hair-win." Allison gave Erin a sleepy smile.

Erin grinned back and waved to Allison as Jared scooped the adorable toddler up to put her down for her nap. Then Erin was alone in Jared's huge but comfortable family room, still nearly reeling from her intimate, revealing glimpse into his personal life.

It was abundantly clear that Jared was as far from Brent as he could possibly be. And while that was a good thing, an uneasy feeling had settled in the pit of Erin's stomach like a lead weight. Jared was, without a doubt, her dream man, the one who made lunch with a toddler propped on his hip, read stories to said toddler over and over again because he couldn't bear to tell her no, and was more sensitive to someone else's needs than Erin was. He was, in theory, perfect.

With a heavy sigh, she knew she was in big trouble. She looked around the toy-cluttered family room and the messy kitchen and out to the picture-perfect backyard, complete with wooden play structure and huge vegetable garden. A longing built within her, a longing so intense, so real, she almost gasped aloud.

She wanted to belong to this family.

She wanted the man who had created this home. She wanted the guy who hadn't let go of his daughter since he'd come home, the one who told stories in silly voices and sang seventies songs in his car with his dog singing along.

She wanted him to care about her the way he cared about Allison. He looked at Allison with such total devotion beaming from his eyes it nearly made Erin cry. What would it be like to be the recipient of that blind devotion? Only Erin's dad had ever cared about her that way, had ever loved her unconditionally, without high expectations she could never meet.

But that love hadn't lasted.

A deep and telling sadness crept into her. This was a fairy tale she would never fit into, a wonderful haven reserved for some perfect, complete woman. She'd failed as a daughter and hadn't had much more luck as a wife. Jared would see her shortcomings, just like her mother and Brent had.

She should leave now; she really should. But she wouldn't. No, she would allow herself this one day with Jared. One perfect day before she wrapped up her threadbare heart and said goodbye to him forever.

Jared returned and invited her out onto the deck for a glass of lemonade and to enjoy the warm afternoon. She met his warm, dark-cocoa eyes, and her heart expanded. Jared was too wonderfully perfect to walk away from just yet.

She'd do that later.

She followed him outside and sat next to him on a padded deck chair on a cedar deck that seemed to stretch for a mile. A light, warm breeze blew, rustling the surrounding trees, scenting the air with pine and a floral scent Erin couldn't identify. They were totally alone here, seated together in a romantic setting. A perfect place for people in love.

Don't even go there.

She glanced over at Jared and smiled nervously. He flashed a wicked grin. Her heart jumped and she felt the unmistakable currents of attraction running between them like electricity. She took a huge swig of lemonade and hoped she could keep her wits about her.

"I love to come out here and unwind," he said.

Erin looked around the gigantic, perfectly landscaped yard. "I can see why. You've done a beautiful job out here."

She felt him shift next to her. "Thanks. I wanted to create a safe environment for Allison. She loves to play outside."

"You love her a lot, don't you?" she asked, even though the answer was obvious.

"She's the best thing that's ever happened to me."

The familiar longing to be important in someone's life filled Erin again. With practiced skill she shoved it deep inside. "She's very lucky to have you," she whispered, unable to banish the wistful tone from her voice.

"Hey." He reached out and took her hand, stroking her fingers. "What's wrong?"

His voice flowed over her like rough silk, drawing out all the feelings she'd tried so desperately to ignore and hide. Fear. Desperate longing. Regret for what could never be. He sounded as if he really cared about her. How she wished she could drown in his voice and his touch and *him.* But she couldn't allow herself that luxury. Not when she knew Jared's words and touches wouldn't last, when inevitably, searing pain would follow.

"Nothing." She could never share all of that with him.

Jared's other hand caressed her cheek. It was a perfect torture, a touch as light as a puff of cotton yet as deep and true as fire-tipped arrows. She bit back a moan. He pressed her cheek and she fought that urgent pressure. She couldn't let him see her shameful inability to believe in herself.

To rise above Brent's wrenching lessons.

"I hope so." He pressed on her cheek again. "Because try as I might I just can't resist you right now."

She gave in reluctantly and swiveled her head, and then her gaze collided with his and she saw that tender, I-care-for-you look that had her emotions running in circles. She felt herself tumbling, drowning.

His fingers skimmed over her face. "Are you still mad that I jumped all over you at the hospital?"

"No." She shook her head. "I'm not mad about that. I'm…confused."

"About what?"

"About…us." The admission came hard. She was letting the conversation wander too close to a place where she didn't want to go—admitting her true, foolish feelings. "We talked at the picnic about why we can't be together…."

He moved nearer, so near his taut leg pressed against hers. "That's true. But I'm having trouble remembering that."

She closed her eyes, trying to ignore how close he was and the heat and want building in her. "So am I."

"Good." He put his arm around her and pulled her close, then reached up and gently pulled her glasses off and set them down on the rustic wooden table next to the chair. Her stomach tumbled and clenched with…anxiety? Excitement? Anticipation?

"Let's do this instead." He dipped his head and pressed a warm, lingering, lemonade-scented kiss on her cheek. "Or maybe this?" He kissed his way back across her cheek to her mouth. His lips caressed hers, then pressed deeper, harder.

Erin opened her mouth and kissed him back. Yes, she could deal with physical attraction. Letting down her guard emotionally…out of the question.

There was no fighting his touch, his kiss, the heaven she always found in his arms. It was a deep, searching kiss, the kind that awakened tendrils of fire in her belly and a longing so deep she didn't think she'd ever be able to fight him. Oh, how she wanted to lose herself in his kiss, despite the reservations and doubts fluttering around her hazy mind like butterflies on the breeze.

With a sigh she pulled him closer, kissed him deeper. A tiny voice of caution hovered on the edge of her consciousness, but she mentally flicked the voice away like a pesky bug and concentrated on the heavenly sensations pouring through her. The feel of Jared's mouth on hers. His unique, heady scent, all man and just him. The feeling of finally being where she belonged.

It was too much to resist. Good or bad, right or wrong, she wanted him too much to walk away. Leave? No way it was going to happen now.

She'd pay the price later.

Chapter Eight

With Erin's soft, seductive rose scent surrounding him, Jared savored the feel of her soft lips against his and the contentment stealing over him, just as it had when he'd sung seventies tunes in the car with her and they'd eaten fried chicken in the park. She always made him feel so settled, so at ease.

So happy.

Vague alarm bells went off somewhere in the far reaches of his brain, but he ignored them and pulled away to gaze down into her heavy-lidded eyes. "Damn, you feel so good."

Erin smiled at him, a dreamy, pleased smile that clogged his breath in his throat. He could get used to seeing her this happy and relaxed.

"You do, too," she murmured, her voice husky and low. She ran a finger around his lips. "Come over here and kiss me some more."

Fresh sparks exploded at her touch, and the warning bells sounding in his head grew louder and more insistent.

He reluctantly pulled away, needing distance from her intoxicating rose scent and sweet kisses. He had to keep things under control. "Erin, honey, I would love to kiss you, but I'd rather talk."

She jerked her head back. "About what?"

He smoothed her silky hair back from her face. "You."

A shadow fell across her face. "Why?"

"Why? Because...I just do."

She let out a puff of air, then flopped back to her own space on her chair. "What do you want to know?"

He shrugged, fighting off a mild sense of anxiety. "Why don't you tell me about your childhood."

"I was a kid, I grew up." She reached for him. "Now come back here and kiss me."

His mild anxiety grew into a hard lump of worry in his chest. He wanted to talk and she was shutting him out the way his father always had. He'd never known how to fight that. "Erin, I'd like to talk."

She abruptly stood and began to pace. "Talking is hard for me," she said, wringing her hands.

"Why?" he asked, wondering why she was so upset.

She stopped pacing and shrugged her slim shoulders. "What if you don't like what you hear?"

The quiet question almost broke his heart. He stood and walked closer to her. "Why do you think I might not like what I hear?"

She looked away, her lip clamped between her teeth, and grasped the chain around her neck. "I don't know."

He pulled on her shoulder. "Yes, you do."

She resisted for a moment, then gave in and faced him, her eyes reflecting a dark, intense pain. "Don't make me talk about this."

"About what?"

"My failings," she said under her breath. "All of the reasons this is wrong."

His heart shriveled a little at the word *wrong*. "What reasons, Erin?" He ran a finger down her silky cheek. "Tell me."

"I'm so afraid of this…this kind of thing. My husband had an affair with one of my friends, ran off with her and left me with huge, devastating debts."

His gaze honed in on her fingers still clamped to the chain around her neck. "Why do you keep grabbing that chain?"

"It's a reminder."

"Of what?"

"Of how careful I need to be. When I was eight, my dad gave me his mother's sapphire ring. I thought the deep-blue sapphire, the tiny diamonds surrounding it, and the delicate, gold filigree setting were beautiful, something fit for a princess. Of course, the ring was too big for me, so I bought this chain at the drugstore so I could wear it around my neck."

She took a deep, shaky breath, and her eyes shimmered with moisture in the sunlight. "Daddy raced his Mustang a week later and swerved to avoid a car turning into his path. He hit a tree and died on the scene." She gave him a sad smile. "I thought he loved me, but after he died in such a senseless, preventable accident, I knew he couldn't have."

His heart nearly broke when he thought of Erin as a bewildered little girl who'd lost her father, and how traumatic it must have been for her when he left her. He reached up and caressed her silky cheek. "What happened to the ring?"

She snorted under her breath. "My mom pawned it."

An ache filled him for all the losses Erin had suffered,

for what her mom had put her through. "So you wear the chain because it reminds you of how much your father hurt you by leaving you?"

She nodded slowly. "Exactly. It helps me to remember how every man I've ever cared about has left me."

He stared at her, unable to breathe, and all of his own fears about love and commitment roared through him like fire. He understood and empathized with her fears perfectly. Too damn perfectly.

Before he could say anything, she asked, "As long as we're talking, what about you? Why haven't you ever married?"

He paced away, his jaw clenched, uncomfortable being the one in the hot seat. "Relationships come with a price."

A long silence stretched out. He sighed inwardly, frustrated. How had this conversation come around to him and his feelings? And how had he let himself get so close to Erin after vowing to keep her from getting under his skin? He was drawn to her in a way he didn't understand, in a way that scared the hell out of him.

She broke the heavy silence. "Why are you so certain you'd pay a price to be with me?"

He jerked his watch on his arm. "I learned early on from my father, and all of the women in his life, that love comes with strings and conditions attached. Allison is the only person who will love me unconditionally."

She looked at him, her leaf-green eyes shrewd. "Maybe so. But will the love of a child be able to fulfill your emotional needs? What happens when Allison grows up and moves away?"

Her unexpected questions scalded him from the inside out, stirring up fiery, painful doubts he hated. "Outside of Allison, I don't have any emotional needs," he said, as much to himself as to Erin. He'd make sure of it.

She stood silently, but he was sure he saw her head shaking slightly. "You're right, then. Strings. Pain…" She left her thought unfinished.

His chest pulled tight. He'd like to beat up the men, and the mother, who'd taught Erin about the pain attached to love. He dropped into the chair in back of him and rubbed the bridge of his nose, feeling a pull between his desire to have Erin near and his instinctive need to remain safe.

Push, pull, over and over. Ignoring his need to be close to her was wearing him down. He was damn tired of fighting his desire.

Maybe he was overanalyzing everything, making this more difficult and complicated than it needed to be. He enjoyed Erin's company. She was funny, smart and attractive. Spending time with her now didn't have to mean lifetime commitment, did it? Why couldn't he enjoy this for the here and now, especially since Erin had made it clear she wasn't in this for the long run?

Viewed from the right perspective, she was the perfect woman for him to spend time with.

He stood and moved toward her, shoving away the niggling notion that his reasoning was flawed, and put his hands on her shoulders. "You had the right idea. Let's not talk anymore, okay?" Pulling her closer, he kissed her again, savoring the feel of her soft body in his arms and losing himself in her rose scent.

She didn't argue. Oh, no. She wrapped her arms around his waist and kissed him back until his head spun and his heart raced and he could barely breathe.

Their conversation and all of his fears faded from his mind, and he lost himself in Erin's seductive scent and her kisses and how good she made him feel. As long as he found himself again eventually, he'd be just fine.

Wouldn't he?

* * *

Erin returned to her office later that afternoon, reeling from the time she'd spent with Jared, locked in his arms, kissing him until she didn't know where she ended and he began.

Heavens. She wanted the man she'd seen this afternoon. Desperately. Could she let herself walk out on that frightening, unstable limb again? Maybe the risk would be worth it for a wonderful man like Jared. The thought of having him and Allison in her life filled her with a compelling, wonderful sense of pleasure she'd never, ever felt.

She plopped down in the chair in Joe's office, envisioning her and Jared and Allison as a family—

Joe's booming voice cut off her fantasy. "Well? You were sure gone a long time. Did you get the story?"

A chill crept up her spine. Darn it all. She'd forgotten all about the story.

"Uh, well, no…"

"Warfield wasn't there?"

She started to fidget. "He was."

"Then why didn't you get the story?"

"I couldn't do it."

"Couldn't or wouldn't?"

She pulled in a deep breath, unable to lie. "Wouldn't."

He stared at Erin, shook his head, then ran a hand over his bald head. "Clean out your desk," he muttered. "I'll send your last paycheck in the mail."

Erin sank back into the chair. Joe had fired her. Refusing to write a story was tantamount to treason to him, and she couldn't tell him that her personal feelings had killed the journalistic fire in her gut. He'd probably go into an apoplectic fit and keel over dead if she told him that.

No, she wouldn't explain anything to Joe, didn't need to. She'd done the right thing, had known it since she'd seen Jared at the hospital, wiped out and worried, and he'd unloaded on her.

Since he'd pulled her into his arms and she'd never wanted to leave.

She drew in a deep, calming breath. "Fine. I'll do that now." She stood on shaking legs, turned and put her hand on the doorknob.

"Erin."

She stopped, her head bent, a whisper of foolish hope still inside of her.

"I'm sorry, but I can't cut you any slack. I've got three reporters willing to do whatever it takes to get the scoop." He paused. "Good journalists don't wienie out for any reason. Ever."

His words slashed at her. All she'd wanted to be since Brent had left her was a good journalist. Now she'd failed at that and disappointed her boss.

But she'd done the right thing by Jared, done the compassionate, ethical thing. She protected him and his family. A tentative rosy glow spread through her, warming the cold spot the loss of her job had caused. Jared trusted her. He'd shared a small slice of his life with her and had held her in his arms. Hopefully that would be enough to get her through this crisis.

Without another word she left Joe's office. When she reached her desk, she stood, staring at nothing for a moment. Even though the rational side of her should be panicking about now, she felt remarkably calm. She was sitting smack-dab in the middle of the highest road on the planet.

Jared had had enough faith in her to not only let down his guard and confide in her about his daughter but to invite her to his home. He'd supported her in front of her mother. The warm, comforting glow she'd felt earlier flared, softening the hard, desperate edge of her sudden unemployment.

Hope rose in her, and for the first time since she'd met Jared, she allowed it to fully bloom and held the feeling close to her heart with both hands.

Jared had proven that he was a wonderful man any woman would be lucky to have.

Maybe he *was* more than just a guy she'd interviewed for a story. Maybe, just maybe, they had a chance.

After Erin cleaned out her desk and took the boxes to her car, the ramifications of losing her job had begun to sink in, despite her warm, fuzzy feelings and hope about a future with Jared. She needed to soften the blow of losing her job by being with him.

So, an hour later, she walked from her office to the nearest Warfield's, hoping to see Jared. She'd used her familiarity with Jared's secretary, Jill, and had managed to convince her to tell Erin where to find Jared. According to Jill, he would be spending the rest of the day at home— with Allison, of course, although Jill hadn't given her a reason—but was going to be at the downtown store briefly this afternoon to handle a problem that had arisen.

Lucky Erin.

She opened the door to Warfield's and stepped inside, loving the way the smell of coffee reminded her of Jared.

She eagerly cast her gaze around, looking for his familiar face. She spotted him behind the counter, dressed in a red, short-sleeved knit shirt and jeans, a white apron tied around his waist. He was obviously helping out again.

She stared for a long moment, struck again by his masculine good looks, how thoroughly attractive and sexy she found him. Her chest tightened, and when he smiled and laughed at someone on the other side of the counter, Erin's knees went weak.

Boy, did she have it bad. Or very good.

Smiling, she started toward him…and stopped abruptly, her blood turning to ice. Jared was laughing with a tall, gorgeous blonde dressed in a tight, above-the-knee skirt, white silk blouse, and high black heels that made her legs look about a mile long.

The blonde was laughing, too, her straight, white teeth glaring. She waved her hand, beckoning Jared out from behind the counter. Jared nodded, took off the apron and stepped around the counter toward the woman.

Blondie put her arm around Jared's broad shoulders, leaned in and said something into his ear, and Jared laughed again. The two of them walked to the door at the back of the store, deep in happy conversation, and disappeared from Erin's view.

Erin stood frozen, her soul aching, her eyes burning with sudden tears. Her chest filled with numbing frost. Her hopes flopped over and died, crushed to death by the sight of Jared taking off with another woman—just the way Brent had.

Idiot.

She reached up and latched on to the chain around her neck. What in heaven's name had convinced her to ignore her common sense and actually believe that she and Jared had a chance, that he was anything more than just some bachelor she'd interviewed for a story? She'd actually glossed over the terrifying, awful fact that she'd lost her job because she'd been happy that Jared had *trusted* her.

What had she been thinking? How had she let herself be sucked into actually believing Jared cared about her? How had she forgotten Brent's brutal tutorial on the pain of pinning her hopes on a man?

She stepped back outside, barely noticing that it had started to rain, needing to get away from the now cloying scent of coffee. She had no earthly idea how she'd fallen into the same old sharp-clawed, vicious trap, but she would figure it out and make darn sure it never, ever happened again.

Chapter Nine

"What the hell…?"

Jared stood in his kitchen the next morning, scanning the headline plastered across the front page of the *Beacon*.

Bachelor Hunk Jared Warfield's Daughter in Hospital
Negligence Suspected

Hot, burning fire filled his chest. He'd trusted Erin, had allowed her into his and Allison's life. And Erin had betrayed him.

His fingers curled around the paper as he skimmed the rest of the story. It was short and to the point. Allison Warfield in the hospital. Negligent nanny. Movie star Janet Worthington and tycoon Angus Warfield's granddaughter. Jared Warfield's adopted daughter. Child's mother died in drug-related motorcycle crash.

Yeah, Erin had done herself proud. She'd taken what he'd told her in confidence and made a front-page, trashy little story out of it.

He let out a heavy breath. She'd slithered her way into his life, shared a couple of kisses, then figured she could capitalize on knowing him and nab a juicy story.

He ran an impatient hand through his hair and swiveled his watch on his arm. He didn't need this right now. Now the press would descend in hordes, and keeping Allison from being on the front page would be hell. By trusting Erin and letting his attraction overwhelm him he'd failed Allison the same way he'd failed Carolyn. Sharp blades of anxiety and anger chopped through his stomach.

"Hi, Dada!"

He turned around and saw Allison, still bleary-eyed from sleep, standing in the doorway to the kitchen dressed in yellow footie pj's, her ragged, stuffed Eeyore clamped in her chubby hand. A white bandage still covered part of her forehead.

His heart melted and his hard-edged anger faded a bit. "Hi, Ally-Bear." He hunkered down and held out his arms. "Come here, pretty girl."

She smiled the toothy little grin that never failed to warm his heart, then toddled over and stepped into his arms. "Hi, Dada. Kiss?"

He kissed her cheek, buried his head in her baby-shampoo hair and picked her up. His chest filled with intense love for this precious little bundle. "Did you have a good sleep?"

She nodded, then dangled Eeyore by the ear. "'Es. Yore, too."

Mrs. Sloane stepped into the room. She smoothed her gray hair back into its perpetual bun. "Good morning, Mr. Warfield."

"Good morning." He tickled Allison's tummy. "I'm the tickle monster!"

Allison giggled. "No! I icky onser!" She dug her tiny fingers in his chest.

He gave a belly laugh, then playfully held her high in the air, which she always loved. "Help me, help me!" he cried. "Ally-Bear, the tickle monster is getting me!"

She laughed. "I icky onser! I icky onser!"

He and Allison took turns tickling each other, something they did all the time, and Jared once again felt pure love expand in his chest. Allison was all he had. He had to protect her. It was past time to get rid of one Erin James.

He stayed long enough to have cereal and juice with Allison, served at the toddler-size table in the kitchen, letting her daintily feed him cereal bites. And then, with a promise to be home in time for dinner and a story before she went to bed, he enjoyed Allison's sticky, juice-scented kisses and left to go to his office.

While he drove the familiar route to town, he couldn't help but wonder how he'd let himself fall for Erin's cold, calculated plot. He should know by now that letting a woman close was a mistake, that he'd pay the inevitable price.

He'd been a fool to let Erin get under his skin.

Shaking his head, he promised himself to stay away from her. She was bad news in a clever, sexy disguise, trouble in a tiny skirt and spike heels.

And while he obviously desired her physically, that was absolutely it, the only way he wanted her. Which was a good thing. Because as soon as he throttled her for writing the story, he'd kick her out of his life as he should have done weeks ago. Then he would be able to concentrate on building a stable life for Allison out of the spotlight.

With Erin's betrayal burning like acid in his gut, forgetting her would be the easiest thing he'd ever done.

*　*　*

Erin flicked off the VCR, tired of watching old Disney movies, especially since she wouldn't be having the happily-ever-after most of them ended with, not to mention that she really didn't have the luxury of sitting around doing nothing.

After paying off Brent's debts, she had enough money in her savings account to last a week or two. The new alternator in her car had depleted her meager savings to almost nothing. She had to find another job quick, but had decided to allow herself one day to regroup before she contacted the few prospects she'd scrounged up in yesterday's paper.

Feeling at odds with nothing productive to do, she rose from the couch, worn-out. But going back to bed would be pointless. She hadn't been able to sleep at all since she'd seen Jared and the blonde at Warfield's yesterday, hadn't been able to do much of anything but sit around and wonder when her brain had quit functioning.

The doorbell rang, and her heart gave a little bounce. Jared? "Yeah, right," she muttered under her breath.

Her hopes deflated and dread kicked in when she looked through the peephole and saw her mom standing on her porch.

Oh, lovely. Just what she needed right now—a visit from the dragon lady. She bit her lip and considered not opening the door. But she discarded the idea; her mom *had* been making an effort lately to improve their relationship, and Erin should try to be a dutiful daughter and meet her halfway, especially since her mom was going through a rough time.

Sighing in resignation, she yanked the door open. "Hi, Mom."

Her mom stepped into the house, glancing at Erin's rumpled, mismatched sweatpants and nightgown. She gave

Erin her usual tight-lipped smile. "Really, dear, you should try to wear nicer clothes. You never know who might show up."

Yeah, like her knight in shining armor was going to come knocking on her door anytime soon.

"Okay, Mom," she said out of habit. "What's up?" Oh heavens, was her mom going to start in on her about Erin's supposedly sleazy boyfriend? Wanda had been too offended by Jared's award-winning performance at the restaurant to say anything about it right afterward.

Her mom sniffed the air, which held the smell of the overcooked pancakes Erin had attempted to make earlier, and held up a bag. "I know what a terrible cook you are, so I thought I'd just drop by some of my low-fat, stuffed cabbage rolls." She let her eyes wander over Erin again and pursed her perfectly painted lips in what she considered a smile. She patted Erin's arm. "A low-fat diet will help you lose some of that extra weight, dear."

Erin ground her back teeth together but was relieved her mom hadn't brought up Jared.

Her mom wandered into the kitchen, making herself at home just as she usually did. "I'll just put this in the refrigerator—oh, my." She popped her head around the doorway to the kitchen, her tastefully made-up blue eyes wide. "Your refrigerator is a mess." She shrugged out of her ancient blue car coat, rolled up the sleeves of her inexpensive but refined cotton-blend blouse and plopped her hands on her imitation linen-clad hips. "It will only take me an hour or so to clean."

Erin stared into the kitchen, her hands clenched at her sides. What would it be like to take Jared's advice and march in and tell her mom to drop the spray cleaner and get the heck out of her kitchen? It would be wonderful.

But old habits die hard, even though Erin hated how her

mom always whirled into her life and managed to make her feel like an incompetent little girl. She'd never managed to stand up to the woman, who was a weird combination of June Cleaver and Atilla the Hun. Scary.

Wanda proceeded to bustle around Erin's kitchen, gathering her trusty cleaning supplies and unloading the refrigerator. Erin let her bustle and clean and mutter under her breath because she didn't want to get into it with her mom, who viewed it as her personal responsibility to keep Erin's appliances sparkling clean.

Why was that? In the past, Erin had just assumed that her mom liked to put her down, but lately she'd sensed something more underneath her mom's constant criticism and compulsive "helping," something akin to a twisted sense of…caring?

Erin rolled her eyes, wandered into the living room and picked up the classified section of yesterday's newspaper to scan the Help Wanted ads.

The doorbell rang again. Her heart did another little Jared jump, but she ignored it and walked over and opened the door. Why was she suddenly so popular? "Hey, Colleen."

Colleen stepped into the house and eyed Erin as if she had the plague. "Yuck. You look awful."

"Why, thank you so much. I've heard that comment about my clothes twice today." Erin closed the door, then glanced down at her faded, navy-blue sweatpants, Mickey Mouse nightgown and bunny slippers. "I guess my outfit matches my mood. Blah."

Colleen sniffed the air and wrinkled her nose. "What's that horrid smell?"

"Burned pancakes."

Colleen shrugged out of her black leather coat. "When are you going to learn to cook?"

"Why in the world is everyone so concerned with my cooking abilities?"

Colleen made a face. "Obviously, that car out front would be your mom's."

"Yup."

As if to confirm that statement, Wanda popped her head around the kitchen door and looked at Colleen. "Oh, it's you." She rolled her eyes. "At least you're not the trash thief."

When Wanda had pulled her head back into the kitchen, Colleen raised her dark blond brows high and said, "Trash thief?"

Erin waved her hands in front of herself. "Don't even ask."

"Okay, I won't." Colleen threw her coat on a small chair. "I know you don't have a subscription and usually bring the paper home from work, so I brought this." She held up a copy of the *Beacon.* "Take a look," she said ominously.

Erin took the paper from Colleen. She cast her gaze down, and dread slid through her like a sly snake. Front and center was an article about Allison Warfield's fall.

Chewing on her lip, she scanned the article. Stan Kempinski, Joe's most recent hire, had taken what little everyone already knew—Allison's well-known family, the tragic circumstances of her mother's death—and embellished it to create what looked like a new, fresh story about a negligent nanny.

"Jared is gonna be livid." Erin threw the paper on the couch, an uneasy depression pressing on her.

Colleen shrugged. "The wheels of journalism move on."

"I think you mean the wheels of justice."

"Whatever. Did he really think he could keep this under wraps?"

Erin flopped onto the couch and rubbed her gritty eyes. "He probably figured the story started and ended with me." She gave a rueful laugh. "Apparently he underestimated the power of the press. When in doubt, make something up."

"Stan had a source."

Erin's gaze flew to Colleen's, her journalistic instincts belatedly firing up. "He did? Who?"

"Get this. Stan didn't even try to contact Jared after Stan read up on Jared's past encounters with the press."

Erin leaned forward. "So, how did Stan get the facts?"

"Some janitor at the hospital was willing to talk."

Erin snapped her eyebrows together. Of course. The janitor mopping the hall around them. She snorted in disgust. "He was nearby when Jared told me everything."

"So you had all the necessary info but you didn't write the story," Colleen offered knowingly.

"I chose not to."

"Because?"

"I made a moral choice, simple as that, and honored a promise. His sweet little girl was in the hospital. Jared was understandably stressed out. Don't they have the right to live their lives privately, without the whole city looking at them, judging?"

Colleen arched a delicate brow at her. "Geez, what's come over you?"

"What do you mean?"

"We're *reporters*. We don't think about things like privacy."

"Well, this time I did." So far Erin hadn't had to worry much about how her stories affected people. Human-interest articles about births at the zoo didn't offend or affect anybody in a negative way. This question of ethics was a whole new thing for her.

Erin picked at a nub on the couch. "Maybe I'm not cut out to be a real reporter."

Colleen leaned forward. "Oh, I think you've got what it takes." She picked the paper up from the floor. "I think it's the subject matter, girl. Warfield has you running in circles about basic stuff. He must be pretty darn special."

Yeah, maybe to the blonde. "Special? No way. Brent was special at first, too, but quickly turned ugly. No." She shook her head. "Special just doesn't last."

"How do you know if you don't give it a chance?" Colleen asked.

"I just do," Erin said with the authority of a woman who had learned her lessons in love the hard, heartbreaking way. Twice. Three times if she threw her father into the mix.

Colleen changed the subject and began babbling about some guy she'd met at the car wash that afternoon, wisely heeding the wisdom of not arguing with Erin. But Erin tuned her out, allowing herself one last dream of everlasting love.

She and Jared and Allison spending the rest of their days together. Building a home for their family, deliriously happy, in love for ever and ever. Her heart safe and whole…

"Erin?" Colleen touched her shoulder. "Earth to Erin."

Colleen jerked Erin from her daydream. "Huh? What?"

"Where did you go?"

Heaven. But heaven didn't exist, did it? "Oh. I…uh, I was just thinking."

Colleen began talking again, and Erin let her drone on in the background while the plain, unvarnished truth sat like a giant elephant on top of her heart. She could dream all she wanted, could envision a happy, love-filled life with Jared and Allison, but after she'd seen Jared and the blonde, what she should have known all along couldn't be ignored or somehow explained away.

It was time to accept the truth. Her foolish, far-fetched dreams would never come true.

Two hours later, after her mom and Colleen had left, a loud pounding sounded on Erin's front door.

Frowning, she went to the door and looked out the peephole. Her stomach dropped.

Jared.

Clutching a newspaper in his hand.

Glaring tawny fire.

Obviously, he'd seen the story about Allison and was justifiably angry about it. Had he come here to commiserate? To seek comfort? Her stomach somersaulted.

Curious and ridiculously hopeful, she opened the door slowly, trying to harden her heart and remember that just yesterday she'd seen Jared with another woman.

He shoved the door open.

"Hey!" She stumbled back a step.

He stepped inside and flung the newspaper at her feet. "You just had to write this story, didn't you?"

She drew in her chin. "Jared—"

"There have been at least eight reporters tailing me all day, salivating for an interview. I told you this would happen, but you went and wrote the stupid thing, anyway."

As realization dawned on her, a cold ball of ice filled her chest. He thought she'd written the story, even though the byline clearly stated that she hadn't.

Darn him, anyway. He'd jumped to the no-brainer, off-base conclusion that she'd broken her word and written the story plastered across the front page of the *Beacon*.

Just like Brent, he'd automatically thought the worst of her, never bothering to give her the credit, or trust, she deserved.

Heartsick and numb, she picked the paper off the floor, tired of trying to prove herself to men who would never, ever believe in her. The question of the day clawed at her. Why had she ignored her gut instincts and let Jared into her life?

She whacked him in the stomach with the paper. "Get out."

He stepped back, staring, and gave an uneasy-sounding laugh. "You're throwing me out?"

She walked over to the door and opened it. "You bet, buster. I'm not going to get into it with you about this. You caught me. I'm a sleazy journalist out to get you. End of story. There's nothing more to discuss."

He stared at her, his eyes reflecting sudden confusion, like maybe he'd hoped that she hadn't written the article. She wanted to laugh. She hadn't written it, but he was too stubborn and uptight and caught up in his own little world to see the truth right in front of him.

He narrowed his eyes. "So you admit you did this?" He shook the paper in the air. "You admit you broke your word and wrote this trash?"

"I don't have to admit anything, Jared. Even though I've never given you a reason not to trust me, you've already decided that I'm someone who can't be trusted." Her eyes burned, and she looked away and bit her lip, praying she wouldn't break down in front of him. "Just get out and take your judgmental, untrusting attitude with you. I've had enough of it."

He looked at her again as if he couldn't quite believe what was happening, as if he was disappointed that she hadn't denied writing the story, as if he'd made a big mistake. Funny thing was, he *had* made a huge mistake. But he was so determined to jam her into his sleazy-reporter mold he couldn't see that she hadn't broken her word.

Not that he should have to depend on some byline to trust her.

"What?" she snapped. "Why are you standing there looking like you can't believe what's happened? I've just confirmed what you've known all along. You should be happy."

With a shake of his head, he moved toward the door, his jaw rigid. "Yeah, well, I'm not. I thought I could trust you, Erin. I told you things in confidence, and you exploited it for your own gain. I guess I just thought that you might at least be a little ashamed."

When he reached the door, he stopped and looked at her. "Frankly, I'm disappointed."

He was disappointed? Ha! He didn't know the meaning of the word, didn't know how it felt to be unfairly judged and convicted like everyone in her life had done to her. She ignored the dull pain knifing through her and then looked right into his eyes and slowly shook her head back and forth. "Believe me, so am I." She would never let him know how much.

He looked away for a long moment, and she could tell that he was trying to figure out how and why she'd turned out to be exactly what he'd feared she would be—someone who would take advantage of him. She supposed she should take some small measure of comfort in the fact that he was surprised at what he'd discovered, that it seemed like it bothered him.

But she found no comfort in that.

He didn't trust her.

A deep, abiding sense of disappointment filled her. Oh, how she wanted to shove the paper under his nose and triumphantly point out the byline, proving to him that he *could* trust her. But she bit her lip and clenched her hands into fists, refusing to say the words that would clear her in his mind.

Her pride wouldn't allow her to show him the truth.

"What are you waiting for?" Why didn't he just leave if he was so disgusted with her?

He shook his head. "I thought you were different." He gave a laugh devoid of humor and jerked on his watch. "I should have known better than to think that."

His words cut her heart into bleeding ribbons. She shoved the searing pain away, unwilling to let his inability to believe in her affect her right now. "I *am* different, Jared." She grabbed the chain around her neck and hung on for dear life. "You're so damn blind you can't see the truth when it's staring right at you."

He stepped away. "The truth?" He swung a razor-sharp gaze to her. "The truth is you betrayed me. That's all I see."

"Yes. That's all you see, all you know. So I guess there's nothing more to say." She stepped back into the house, ignoring how her knees shook, and gave him a dispassionate stare. "Goodbye, Jared."

He looked at her again, and she could have sworn she saw a glimmer of regret in his coffee-colored eyes. But it was gone in an instant, and she decided she'd imagined it. He would undoubtedly *not* regret that she'd turned out to be exactly what he'd been trying to make her into all along—a sleazy reporter. He could easily walk away now, secure in the knowledge that she wasn't worthy of his trust.

How convenient for him.

"Goodbye, Erin," he said, his voice oddly soft. He then turned and walked down the cement porch steps without looking back.

He opened his car door, threw the newspaper onto the passenger side floor, sat down, closed the door and started the engine. He slowly backed out of her driveway without looking at her. She wanted to turn away, but she didn't. She forced herself to watch him drive out of her life, her tattered heart crumbling, ensuring that she would accept without reservations that she would never see him again.

And then he was gone.

A profound sadness engulfed her for the second time in two days, a sadness for the death of a foolish dream she'd sworn she'd never let herself indulge in again. Her eyes burned, but she refused to cry and let his inability to trust her, to see the real her, cut too deep.

She sank down onto the porch. Deep down she absolutely hated to admit that Jared had wormed his way into her heart enough for the cut to matter. She hated to admit that the pain his brutal assumptions and distrust had caused came so close to the pain she'd felt when her dad had risked his life and left her.

But what Jared had done *did* hurt almost as much as when her dad had foolishly died. Oh, heavens, it did.

Late that night, long after midnight, Jared sat in the dark in the oak rocker in Allison's room, rocking her back to sleep after she'd awakened, crying. Her even, deep breathing told him she'd fallen asleep, but he didn't put her back into her crib. He wanted to hold his little girl, feel her pajama-clad, chubby body in his arms and remind himself what was important in his life, who would love him unconditionally, who would never betray him.

Allison.

He pressed his face into her satiny curls and touched her soft-as-cotton cheek, trying to focus on her baby-scented skin instead of letting himself dwell on Erin.

But it didn't work. He'd held off the memories all day, choosing to spend the evening playing tea party with Allison rather than dwell on what had happened at Erin's. But now, with the world quiet around him and the darkness somehow amplifying his every thought, he couldn't shut his mind down.

With a muffled oath he allowed his thoughts of Erin free rein in his mind. Strangely, instead of remembering how she'd betrayed him, he recalled the hurt look on her face when he'd stepped into her house, waving that damn newspaper around. Pain had flashed in her eyes several times, an unexpected pain that had slashed him to the core, despite what she'd done by writing that horrible story.

Why did he have the feeling that he'd somehow stepped into the middle of a movie? And why did he feel as if he'd made some sort of mistake? She'd freely admitted she'd written the story, hadn't she? Nobody else had access to the information he'd shared with her.

But she'd looked haunted and hurt when she'd confirmed she'd written the piece of trash, and her voice had sounded strained and shaky. He'd seen the shadows in her gorgeous green eyes, and he just couldn't forget how shattered, vulnerable and hollow she'd looked.

He rubbed the back of his neck, wishing none of this mattered and that he could just forget about Erin and concentrate on Allison. He really didn't want to wonder and worry about Erin's reaction today. Letting himself dwell on her big, sad eyes would get him nowhere except closer to a complicated, painful, strings-attached relationship he had to avoid.

He pulled Allison closer and closed his eyes, reminding himself that *she* would fill his heart with love, that *she* would never make him pay the price Erin undoubtedly would. Allison was all he needed. Feeling better, he placed her in her crib, kissed her downy cheek and walked back to his room. He looked at his empty, cold bed, the sheets and blankets rumpled on one side and still perfectly made on the other. He froze, staring, suddenly numb.

The other side of his bed would never be rumpled by or hold the warmth of a woman. A cold, hard shaft of doubt pierced him. But he immediately discounted the feeling; he was simply tired and stressed out about everything that had happened in the past few days.

But after he'd climbed into bed, turned out the light and settled in to go back to sleep, his doubts nagged him, keeping him awake far into the night. And even though he hated the thought, he couldn't help but wonder if someday he'd regret that he didn't have anyone to keep the other side of the bed, and his heart, warm.

Chapter Ten

The next day Jared did his level best to forget what had happened at Erin's house and how the sight of the empty, cold side of his bed had bothered him. He ate breakfast with Allison, read her a story, changed her bandage, then left for the office, determined to immerse himself in his daily routine to get Erin out of his head. He diligently worked at his desk all morning, going over the monthly sales figures, hoping against hope that the new numbers would be better than the month before.

But they weren't. Sales were still falling at Warfield's and he had no idea why.

Frustrated, he called a meeting with his department heads and drilled them relentlessly, trying to get to the bottom of whatever was causing the dip in sales.

But an image of Erin, her face sad and full of disappointment, haunted him through the meeting. After he barked some orders, his employees left him alone, and he sat at his desk, staring into space, simply unable to get rid of the crazy thought that he'd somehow made a big mistake.

He couldn't dismiss the red flags Erin's reaction had raised in his brain. And, damn, it was more than simply being upset that she'd so blithely admitted writing the article about Allison. Sure, he'd hated hearing confirmation that she'd betrayed him. He'd hoped that she was different from all of the grasping women who had paraded through his and his father's lives. But the feeling twisting inside of him went deeper than that. Her hurt reaction sliced him to the bone because of its compelling nature. Had she been trying to make some sort of point? If so, what was it?

He jerked his watch on his arm. What was going on?

Finally, after lunch, he decided he needed to see Erin again and clear the air if he was ever going to get any work done. He ignored the spurt of excitement that raced through him when he thought about breathing in her rose scent, seeing her pretty green eyes and hearing her lilting laugh. He was simply going to see her to clarify things in his mind once and for all. Not a big deal.

With that aim in mind, he drove too fast to her office, stole another guy's parking space on the street, parked and made his way to her building. Striding into the lobby of the *Beacon,* he moved toward the small reception area and smiled at the plump, dark-haired young woman behind the polished wood desk. "I'm here to see Erin James. Where is her office located?"

"I'm sorry, sir, Erin James doesn't work here."

He frowned. "Yes, she does. She interviewed me for an article."

"Yes, well, she *did* work here, but she doesn't anymore."

He fell back a step. A sick feeling plunked itself down

and lodged in his belly. "Since when? Why doesn't she work here anymore?"

The young woman shrugged. "I really can't say. I was just told to forward all of her calls to another reporter."

He nodded, his stomach coiling. Had Erin been fired? Or had she quit? Maybe she'd landed a better job because of the scoop she'd written on him.

His gut instinct told him her leaving hadn't been voluntary. She seemed to love her job, and he knew how financially strapped she was. An oily tide of dread slid through him. He closed his eyes briefly and pictured her hollow eyes and quivering lips in his mind. No wonder she'd seemed upset.

Whatever the reason, she was out of a job, and she hadn't said a thing about it yesterday when he'd come down on her so hard. She could have easily thrown that out to garner his sympathy, but she hadn't.

A grudging sense of admiration filled him, and, man, he wanted to go to her and take her in his arms and wipe away the despair he'd seen dulling her eyes yesterday, the despair he couldn't help but feel he'd put there.

As he drove back to his office on autopilot, jumbled thoughts and bits of conversations danced through his brain in fast motion for the millionth time.

I am different, Jared. You're so damn blind you can't even see the truth when it's staring right at you.

She lost her job. Her hurt-filled eyes.

Her brittle, forced smile today.

I've never given you a reason not to trust me....

His mind churning, he reached for the edition of the *Beacon* that he'd flung onto the floor of his car when he'd left Erin's yesterday. His brows knitted together, he perused the story. And finally noticed what he'd been too angry to notice before—the byline.

Stan Kempinski.

The nebulous bit of information he'd been searching for hit him in the head like a line drive to center field.

Erin hadn't written that story.

He almost swerved off the road. Breathing hard, he stomped on the brakes and pulled over, screeching to a stop.

Erin hadn't betrayed him. And she'd lost her job because of it.

The last piece of the puzzle fell into place.

Thick, heavy remorse settled over him. He felt like he had the word *jerk* emblazoned on his forehead. And he deserved it. He'd blustered along like a steamroller and hadn't given Erin the benefit of the doubt. Worse, when he'd stormed over to her house, there hadn't even been a scrap of uncertainty in his mind that she was guilty. And she'd more than likely lost her job because of her choice, because she'd kept her word.

He was an absolute fool.

A hollow, cold sadness filled him. Erin didn't give *her* trust easily, either, and he had handed her a huge reason never to trust him again. Regret pressed on his chest like a gigantic vise. His heart froze, radiating shards of ice into every corner of his body.

And, man, surprisingly, it hurt like hell.

Erin replaced the phone in its cradle and shook her head, wondering about her wacky day. First her mom had called to apologize for criticizing Erin when she'd come to her house the day before. She'd sounded really sorry and had talked of coming for another overnight visit, saying more than once that she missed Erin.

Now another strange, totally unexpected phone call had come Erin's way. Had some weird, cosmic phenomenon zapped her world and twisted her life into something she didn't recognize?

She looked at Colleen. "You are absolutely not going to believe what just happened."

Colleen looked up from the hand she had spread on Erin's oak kitchen table, a nail polish brush tipped in bright red in her other hand. "Do tell."

"That was Joe. Apparently Jared was chosen Favorite Bachelor and he wants me to do another follow-up to 'The Bachelor Chronicles.'"

Colleen frowned and blew on her freshly painted nails. "Joe fired you. You don't work for the *Beacon* anymore."

"I know. That's what's so weird." Erin plopped down into the wood chair across from Colleen. "Joe wants to rehire me. Said he was too hasty firing me and wants me to come back."

Colleen raised a brow. "Are you going to do it?"

Erin bit her lip. "Well, I should, because I need a job and I need the money."

"But?"

"But I'd have to interview Jared again," Erin said, hating the very idea of seeing Jared, under any circumstances.

"Big deal. You're over him right?" Colleen smiled slyly. "Oh, I forgot. You don't need to be over him because you never cared about him, right?"

Erin wanted to sock Colleen in the arm. "Okay, so I did care about him, sort of," she lied. "But after I saw him with that woman and he assumed I wrote that story, I don't anymore." She really didn't.

"So what's the problem? Just interview him and that will be that." Colleen gave her a smug look. "Right?"

"Wrong," Erin muttered. Very wrong. "I don't want to see him again and be reminded of how little trust he had in me. His chapter in my life ended the moment he chose to believe that I betrayed his confidence and wrote that story, and now I just want to move on and forget all about him.'' She chewed on her thumbnail. ''Besides, he'll never agree to talk to me. He thinks I'm a sleaze.''

''But you're not. You didn't write the story. Go tell him that. Maybe he'll agree to help you out.''

Erin stood and began to pace. ''I don't think so. He hates the press, and, I have to tell you, it rubs me the wrong way to have to tell him what he should be able to figure out on his own. How hard is it to simply trust me because I've never given him a reason not to?'' She blew out a fat breath of air. ''But I need my job back and I need to prove to Joe, and myself, that I can be a good journalist.''

Colleen screwed the cap back on the nail polish. ''Maybe you can convince Jared it would benefit him and his business if he agrees to the article.''

''Been there, done that.'' Erin drummed her fingers on the Formica countertop. ''After the article on Allison's nanny being negligent, he'll never agree.''

''He might if he sees it as an opportunity to set the record straight.''

Erin quit drumming her fingers and looked at Colleen. ''You know, you might have something there. Jared has always seen the press as the enemy. Maybe I can convince him otherwise, that the press can serve a purpose—to set the record straight.''

Colleen smiled and winked. ''You go, girl. You'll have him eating out of your hand in no time.''

Erin weakly returned Colleen's grin, wishing she felt as confident about this plan as Colleen obviously did. And while she might, if the planets somehow aligned, convince Jared to agree to be part of another edition of ''The Bachelor Chronicles,'' she was beyond wary of having Mr. Gorgeous Coffee Eyes in her life again. There had been no negative article when he'd been cozying up to that blonde, right after kissing Erin.

The thought of putting herself back in a position where he could hurt her again scared her to death. The wounds of distrust ran deep.

But she had no choice. She needed her job back and she absolutely had to convince Jared to help her out. She had to fight for what she wanted.

And she would be sure to convince him without falling under his potent spell again.

The next morning Erin paused next to Jared's open office door and took a deep breath, trying to calm her racing heart. A strange sense of déjà vu filled her; she remembered a month ago when she'd come here and found Jared tending his rooftop garden and she'd tried to convince him to participate in the original edition of "The Bachelor Chronicles."

New edition, same stubborn, untrusting, thoroughly exasperating man.

You have to do it, Erin.

She'd already negotiated a higher salary and extra perks for returning to the *Beacon*. She was on a roll. It was time to earn that extra money. Her hands shaking, she smoothed her white silk blouse, fluffed her hair—why in the world did she care about her hair?—and told herself to ignore Jared's stunning, coffee-brown eyes and stop-her-heart smile.

This was strictly business.

For the sake of her job she would stuff her pride and tell him she wasn't the author of the article, convince him to consent to another interview, and that would be it. She'd be out of here in ten minutes, tops.

Feeling better, she stepped into the open doorway. And stopped cold. Jared sat at his desk with Allison on his lap. The little girl, dressed in a darling pastel sweat outfit, was playing patty-cake with him.

Erin's heart stalled. Jared had the most contented, ecstatic, love-filled smile on his face as he played with Allison, it almost took the breath from Erin's chest. Heavens, what she would give to have him look at her that way, with pure, unadulterated love shining from his eyes.

Before she could deal with the ramifications of that stupid, staggering wish, Jared shifted his gaze and looked right at her. His dark eyes widened fractionally.

"Erin!" he said, clearly startled by her sudden appearance. A smile crossed his face, and he looked as if he was actually happy to see her.

But then his smile was replaced by a confused, sort of contrite expression and he confirmed that emotion when he said, "Uh, what are you doing here?"

She plastered a brittle smile on her face and managed, somehow, to find her voice. "I need to talk to you."

He put his arms around Allison, putting an end to her singsong rendition of patty-cake. She giggled, then turned around and looked at Erin with the clearest, most innocent blue eyes Erin had ever seen.

"Hi, Hair-Win!" Allison waved a chubby hand. "Pata-cake?"

Erin smiled, enthralled by the adorable toddler. "Yes, I see you're playing patty-cake." She took a few tentative steps into the office. "Is that your favorite game?"

"'Es, 'tis." She patted both tiny hands on Jared's whisker-shadowed cheeks. "Dada, too."

Jared nodded. "Yes, Ally-Bear, me, too."

Allison continued to gently pat Jared's cheeks. Jared tweaked her button nose and indulgently let her continue, then looked at Erin. "Allison's nanny had an appointment, so Allison is staying with me for a while."

"Oh." Erin was surprised he was sharing that information with her, since she was a slimy reporter and all.

"Actually, I'm glad to see you." He awkwardly leaned forward and cleared his throat. "I've been wanting to talk to you, but haven't…had the time."

She stared at him. "Really?" she said, trying to mask her total astonishment. Wasn't he still angry about how she'd *betrayed* him?

He took Allison's hands in his. "Yes, really. But I have to meet Mrs. Sloane in a few minutes. Are you free for dinner?"

An arrow of excitement shot through Erin, but she squashed the ridiculous reaction and schooled her features into a bland expression, determined to keep her reactions to him on a business level only. "Yes, actually, I am." She would eat dinner with him on the moon if it meant gaining his cooperation.

"Good. I usually have an early dinner with Allison and put her to bed, so I'll pick you up at seven-thirty."

No way. This was a business meeting, period. And that meant she would meet him at the restaurant instead of giving in to her stupid dreams and allowing him to pick her up at her house the way he would do if they meant anything to each other.

She held up a hand. "I'll just meet you at the restaurant, okay?"

He snagged her eyes with his surprised, mocha gaze and looked like he was about to insist on picking her up. But then, obviously, he realized that the regular dating rules didn't apply. "Okay. Chez Maurice, at seven-thirty, then?"

"That's fine. I'll see you then." She nodded, then

turned and walked from his office, her hopes for her job, and self-respect, on the rise.

She'd swallowed her fears, faced Jared and had another chance to snag her story. She wasn't dead in the water yet. She'd take what she could get and be darn glad for it.

Funny how that didn't seem like enough.

Chapter Eleven

Erin waited for Jared at the table at Chez Maurice, a swanky restaurant in the Pearl District in northwest Portland, trying not to fidget, sternly reminding herself this wasn't a date so she had no earthly reason to be nervous. Not that she should need a reminder after Jared had shown her that he had no faith in her, just like Brent.

She was through being wounded, through letting other people walk all over her.

It was time to take care of herself, to nurture her growing sense of self-respect.

A second later she spotted Jared walking through the dimly lit restaurant toward her, looking absolutely gorgeous in a black suit, white dress shirt and paisley tie that complemented his dark hair and coloring perfectly. He moved with an easy male grace that sent hot chills skittering up and down her spine, radiating heat into her body.

Just tell him I didn't write the story, secure his cooperation and leave.

To distract herself, she jerked her recorder and pad of

paper out of her briefcase, ready to get her story and get this...thing with Jared over with.

For good.

He arrived at the table and smiled awkwardly, his eyes reflecting something she couldn't quite identify, something she'd picked up on when she'd seen him at his office earlier today. Strange. In the past he'd always seemed to be in such perfect control of his emotions.

"Erin," he murmured, unbuttoning his suit jacket. He pulled out his chair and sat down. "Sorry I'm late."

"No problem."

He looked at her for a long moment, saying nothing, then he picked up his cut-crystal water glass and drank half of it down.

Alarms went off in her head. Something wasn't right. He was on edge and nervous, which wasn't like him at all. Unable to help herself, she shook her foot under the table and drummed her fingers on the linen-covered table, getting ready to ask for another interview.

Before she could speak, Jared said, "I...ah, well, I guess I owe you an apology."

She raised her eyebrows. "You do?"

He reached out and took her trembling fingers in his big, warm hand. "Yes, I do." He shook his head and looked down for a moment. "You didn't write that story."

She froze, trying to separate how good his hand felt wrapped around hers from the astonishment crashing through her. She opened her mouth to speak but no sound would come out.

"I can see I've caught you by surprise," he said dryly.

She gathered her wits about her and pulled her hand from his. "Uh, well, yes, you have." She smiled tightly. "You finally bothered to check the byline."

"Yes." He pinned her with his clear, coffee-shaded eyes. "I know now you would never betray me like that."

She glared at him, ignoring how his eyes sent shivers down her spine. "*Now* being the key word. Yesterday was a different story. You were very, very sure I'd deliberately done a hatchet job on you, even though I promised I wouldn't." She took a breath, wondering how much she should vent. She *was* going to have to ask him—no, demand—for his cooperation in a few minutes. But her wounded pride and her new, painfully acquired backbone wouldn't let her stuff her feelings. She continued on, building steam, and said, "You assumed the worst about me, like most of the people in my life. That hurt."

"Erin, please try to understand. I saw the story and was mad and read it without paying much attention. And you *were* the only one I'd talked to...." He shook his head. "I still don't know how the story got out."

"Remember the janitor mopping the hallway? Apparently, he had very big ears."

He nodded. "Ah."

She shifted in her chair. "I gave you my word, Jared. Didn't that mean anything to you?"

"I...I assumed you had written it, since you came looking for information."

She pointed a rigid finger at him. "No, what happened was that I was trying to protect you and your family, and you automatically thought the worst."

He grimaced. "And you lost your job because of that decision, didn't you?"

She froze, embarrassed that he'd discovered what she'd sacrificed to protect him when he hadn't had one measly iota of trust in her. "Yes, I did."

"I was such an idiot," he said under his breath. "Erin,

I'm sorry I misjudged you. My past makes it difficult for me to trust many people.''

Her curiosity about him exploded. "Why? Why do you distrust me so much? You talk about your past, which I've never even been a part of.'' She looked right into his eyes. "Have I ever given you a reason to doubt my intentions?''

He looked down and fiddled with his fork, refusing to meet her gaze for a moment. Then he looked up, contrition written all over his face. "No, no you haven't. I was way off base, and I've apologized. Let's just leave it at that, all right?''

She hesitated, torn. She should probably do the prudent thing and just let things be, but darn it, he'd really hurt her and she wanted to know why. Maybe she was a glutton for punishment, and maybe he would storm out of the restaurant, leaving her with no story, but for her own peace of mind and growing desire to understand herself she had to know why he'd been so quick to judge her. There was *her* past to consider, too.

"No," she said softly. "It isn't all right. A lot of people in my life have always thought the worst of me. I want to know why I can now count you among them.''

He let out a heavy breath. "I've already told you, the press has always hounded me, and they descended in hordes when my sister Carolyn died.'' A muscle in his jaw twitched. "I've had reporters trying to weasel their way into my life for as long as I can remember, and I want to protect Allison from that.''

She digested what he'd said, understanding why he'd be wary of the press, why he'd want to protect his daughter. Too bad her own dad hadn't been as dedicated. She knew from personal experience how the past could affect one's actions in the present. But his actions seemed to go beyond simple mistrust for the press. "Is that the only reason?" she ventured, sensing that she was treading on thin ice.

He looked at her intently, then jerked on his watch. "Isn't that a good enough one?"

Even though she was dying to pick beneath the surface of the fascinating man sitting across from her, she was a fool to be so interested in him beyond "The Bachelor Chronicles." Keeping things impersonal would keep her safe. And wouldn't ruffle his feathers, which only concerned her because she needed her story. "I suppose it is."

He inclined his head. "That's it, then."

The tuxedoed waiter arrived and took their order, and after he left, an awkward silence fell over the table. Erin bit her lip and fought the urge to chew on her fingernail like a weak-willed teenager. She had to tell Jared about the new edition of "The Bachelor Chronicles" and demand his cooperation. Right now.

She cleared her throat, preparing to act the way Jared would if his job was on the line—with confidence and cold, hard self-assurance. "Actually, Jared, there is something I'd like to talk to you about."

"Fire away."

"My editor called and offered me my job back."

His eyes lit up and he flashed a smile. "Hey! That's great!" He reached over and squeezed her hand. "Things have turned out all right, then."

She pulled her hand away from him again. "There is one tiny requirement, though."

He hoisted a lone brow. "Which is?"

"You've been chosen Best Bachelor, and my editor wants to do another edition of 'The Bachelor Chronicles.'" She paused for effect. "With you as the subject."

His smile faded. "No freakin' way."

"Yes, indeed." She added a trace of steel to her voice. "And after what you've done, I expect you to help me out."

He stared at her, looking shocked, and a surge of power moved through her, lighting up a dark, untouched space inside of her.

And, heavens, she liked being in control.

A healthy dose of raw admiration moved through Jared. Erin was something else, all right, her green eyes as hard as emeralds, using what he'd done to force him to help her out.

He moved his gaze over her, enjoying the view. She looked lovelier than he remembered in a pale-blue, shimmery sweater that hugged her figure and made her red curls look like tawny fire and her green eyes glow like leaves in the sun.

A surge of heat moved through him, and he wanted to take her in his arms and hold her close and drink in the scent and feel of her. Man, he wished he could turn back time and wipe away the assumptions he'd made. Regret pressed in on him.

Before he could respond to her demand, Erin cleared her throat and said, "Can I say something that might make a difference?"

"Have at it," he invited, interested in what she had to say.

"I know you think of the press as the enemy, and with good reason. But I think you should think of 'The Bachelor Chronicles' as an opportunity to set the record straight. You say you trust me now, right?"

He nodded. "I do."

"Well, then trust me to write a story that will give you the opportunity to not only snag publicity for Warfield's, but also give you the chance to correct any misperceptions formed after the story that ran yesterday.''

More admiration shot through him. As he had come to expect, Erin was sharp, and she had certainly made her case well. He steepled his hands in front of himself. ''Warfield's *could* use the publicity, and Mrs. Sloane *was* in no way negligent. I'd like to make that publicly known.'' He looked away.

''So?''

He hesitated, still wary of the damage the press could inflict. ''You would be writing all of the story? And there are no extra 'dates' involved? No offense, but one extra-terrestrial-hunting woman was enough.''

''I'd write the whole story. And no dates.'' Her eyes hardened to flinty green again. ''And I should let you know that I probably have enough information from our previous interviews to write a decent follow-up.'' She sat back, her mouth pressed into a grim line. ''So it's up to you whether you want a hand in this or not. I'll get the job done either way.''

Jared stared at her. Even though she was shoving him between the proverbial rock and a hard place, he couldn't help but like what he saw, couldn't help but be in awe of the strong, go-after-what-she-wanted woman she was. She had turned this situation around to her advantage, playing a winning hand to perfection. Good for her.

And she was dead-on. He did owe her his help after what he'd done, as much as he owed her the gift he had in his pocket. ''You've made your case well. I'd be glad to help you out.''

She inclined her head, a triumphant smile on her face. ''I knew you'd see reason.'' She picked up the recorder and turned it on. ''Let's get started.''

* * *

Feeling victorious, Erin turned off the recorder. She had loads of information to write a fantastic follow-up on Jared. Joe would bow before her in humble appreciation when she turned in this story, she was sure of it. Thank goodness her career was back on track.

In that vein it was well past time to put her personal life back together, too. Luckily her business with Jared was concluded. In fact, everything with Jared was finished. Done. Over with.

This was it.

Determined not to let the notion of never seeing Jared again bother her, she shoved her recorder into her briefcase. "Well, that's it, then." She rose and smiled in a professional way at Jared. "Thanks for your help."

He held up a hand. "Wait. I have something for you."

She widened her eyes and blinked, ignoring how her heart leaped, and dropped back into her chair, her knees suddenly disgustingly weak. "You…you have a gift for me?"

With a flourish, he pulled a small velvet box from his jacket pocket and handed it to her. "Yup. Just for you."

Her hands shaking, she opened the box. She looked down and her jaw literally sagged to her chest. Inside were diamond earrings, each one the size of Maine. She'd need a hoist to put them on. "Oh…my…goodness."

"Look, I thought about what I'd done, thinking you'd written that story and all, and I wanted to get you something to say I was sorry."

She raised wide, disbelieving eyes to his face. For a horrifying second Brent sat across from her wearing a smug, satisfied smile, his hand outstretched. She could just hear him thinking, *I bet this bauble will make it all right.*

Numb, she looked down and stared at the earrings. A raw tide of bitter disappointment and anger shot through her. Jared might have belatedly caught a clue and realized that she hadn't written the story, but this...well this took the prize for unromantic, tactless gestures.

How had she naively thought, even for one tiny moment, that he was presenting her with a token of love?

She wanted to laugh. This didn't have anything to do with love or romance or what lay deep in his heart. He was only apologizing for his brutal assumptions, and in a remarkably insensitive way to boot.

She tightened her jaw and looked at him, noting the hopeful expression on his face. She coldly disregarded the look. "So you figured that you could just buy me off and everything would be okay, right?"

He looked stricken. "No, Erin—"

She shot to her feet and put the velvet box on the table, resisting the urge to throw it at his head. "No, don't say anything. You've done enough already."

Boy, had he.

Without looking back, she picked up her stuff and left the restaurant, a sick feeling lodged like a bad meal in her stomach. Her battered, aching heart had died a little tonight when she'd seen those earrings, when she'd realized something that pierced her to her very soul.

Jared was more like Brent than she'd ever imagined.

Floored and heartsick, Jared watched Erin walk out on him, his chest feeling more hollow with every step she took, one single thought reverberating in his brain:

Go after her.

He threw a couple of bills on the table and jumped to his feet, not stopping to analyze why he couldn't let her go. He simply knew with every instinct in him that he couldn't leave things like this between them.

He hurried across the restaurant, out the door and onto

the street, an urgent, surprising sense of do-or-die filling him. A warm, late-summer breeze blew across his face. He took a sharp breath and looked left and right, catching sight of her rounding the corner down the block on his left.

Setting his jaw, he followed her, catching up to her in the parking lot around the corner from the restaurant. "Erin, wait!"

She dropped her hand from her car door and stood with her head down for a moment. When he reached her, she looked at him, her green eyes unyielding, her mouth pressed together in a hard line. "Jared, leave me alone."

Her words weren't surprising, but they still burned a hole in him a mile wide. "I don't want to leave things like this." He yanked his tie loose and caught her gaze with his. "I've upset you."

She gave a tiny, under-the-breath snort and placed a fisted hand on her hip. "What else is new?"

He cringed inwardly, sick that he'd hurt her twice in two days. He had to fix his mistake—somehow, had to wipe away the flinty look in her normally soft, beautiful eyes. "Okay, I deserved that. But…I didn't mean to. I really thought you'd like the earrings."

"I'm sure you didn't mean to hurt me, but you know what? You did, and that showed me that I can't keep doing this. I can't keep setting myself up for heartache."

The thought of her heart aching over him bothered the hell out of him; he'd caused the pain inside of her like so many other people in her life had.

Panic seeped into him. He'd messed everything up. He reached out and touched her shoulder, then ran his hand down her arm and grasped her small, soft hand. "Okay, I understand that. But don't walk out on me yet…Hair-Win. I have something I want to show you."

She leaned against the car, shook her head and looked at him from the corner of her eyes. A ghost of a smile hovered around her lips. ''You just had to use that name, didn't you? That's hitting pretty low.''

He let go of her and spread his hands wide, slightly relieved by her small smile. ''I'm a practical guy. I'll do whatever it takes.'' He drew in a deep breath. ''Come with me. Please?''

She straightened and pushed her hair behind her ear. She muttered under her breath for a few seconds, then sighed and looked at him. ''All right, all right, I'll come. But only because my mom's at my house and I'd like to avoid her for a while. Don't get any ideas, Warfield. You're still in deep doo-doo.''

''Hey, I'll take whatever I can get. Let's go, then.''

They walked to his car, which was parked around the block on the street. She stayed quiet, and he did, too. A growing sense of doom was building in him, and as much as he didn't want to admit it, that horrible feeling had everything to do with a suddenly frightening prospect, a prospect that, very surprisingly, filled his heart with cold, icy dread.

He could very well end up exactly the way he'd always wanted to be.

Alone.

Chapter Twelve

Erin sat down in Jared's car, wondering if she'd lost her mind by agreeing to come with him. But her mom had mentioned wanting to have a long talk about Erin's choice in men, and Erin would hitch a ride with the Wicked Witch of the West before she'd face *that*. Besides, Jared was a hard guy to resist—he always had been—and his use of Allison's nickname for her had hit Erin right in the middle of her heart.

Determined to make the best of the situation, if that was possible, she said, "So, where are you taking me?"

He lifted a shoulder. "I have something I've been wanting to show you." He leaned toward the car window and scanned the evening sky. "It's the perfect time of day for what I have in mind."

"What's that?"

"It's a surprise." He shifted into reverse and backed out of the parking space. "So, why are you avoiding your mom?"

Erin sighed. "I'm expecting her to come down on me for my taste in boyfriends."

"Oh, man, I'm sorry. You want me to come clean with her?"

"No." She shook her head. "Probably wouldn't make any difference. I've never really been able to please her."

"I know how that is," he said, giving her a sympathetic smile. "My dad was cold and critical, too. Nothing I did was good enough for him."

She shifted in her seat, surprised to hear they had so much in common, which she never would have guessed. Jared seemed so secure and confident in himself. "So, why do you think parents do that?"

He shrugged. "I don't know about your mom, but my dad took after his dad. My grandfather died before I was born, so I never knew him, but I've been told he was a cold man who threw his money around but never told anyone he loved them." He deftly navigated the car onto an off-ramp. "My dad did the same thing."

"Hmm," she murmured thoughtfully. "That part about the money sounds familiar."

"So your mom does that, too?"

"No," she said quietly. "I was talking about you."

He stomped on the brake. The car lurched and the tires squealed, then it jerkily rolled to a stop at the end of the highway off-ramp. "No way." He turned and captured her eyes with his. "You don't mean that, do you?"

"Well, only if you call trying to make me feel better with gigantic diamond earrings throwing your money around." The barb came out a bit harsher than she'd intended, but she'd meant it.

Her candid statement landed like a bomb. "Whoa, whoa. Okay, obviously we've got something to talk about." He accelerated and made a hard left turn. "We're almost there. I want to concentrate on what you have to say, so hold off for a minute or two, and then we can talk. All right?''

''Uh...fine by me.'' She swallowed. A serious conversation? As in a heart-to-heart, this-is-how-I-feel kind of discussion? Heavens, not that! She wasn't any good at that kind of stuff.

Stiffen that lip for once, Erin.

Yes. She was absolutely through letting Jared rattle her; finished running scared around him. This whole situation with him had to end. Tonight. She had to be strong. For herself.

Trying to calm her nerves, Erin asked. ''How's Allison?''

A smile lit his face. ''She's great. She keeps asking about you, Hair-Win. She liked you a lot.''

Her insides warmed, but the knot taking up residence in her stomach prevented further conversation. She sat silently, nibbling on her thumbnail, dreading the coming conversation, even though it had to happen.

After winding up Skyline Boulevard for a few miles, they arrived at a cemetery.

She drew her brows together. ''A cemetery?'' Was he being funny or insulting? Or was his sister buried here?

He parked the car and flashed a smile, his dark, coffee eyes gleaming. ''Not the cemetery. Something *at* the cemetery.'' He unbuckled his seat belt and opened his door. ''Come on.''

Wondering what he was up to, she unbuckled her seat belt and climbed out, filled with a fluttery apprehension she hated.

She joined him as he walked up a narrow gravel path, and a wave of familiar sadness rolled through her. Even though there was an emptiness in her heart that she instinctively knew only Jared could fill, there was also an unhealed wound there, and filling her emptiness wouldn't miraculously heal that gash.

To distract herself, she looked around, noticing the well-kept lawns and shrubbery of the calm cemetery. Fragrant pink geraniums lined one side of the path. Ahead she spied colorful clusters of flowers and lush green bushes near the path.

Dusk was beginning to fall. The early October evening was unseasonably warm, but comfortable, and a soft breeze ruffled her hair. The setting sun lay like a huge, red-orange ball of fire against the backdrop of various shades of pink and lavender layers of clouds. Red streaks shot through the vibrant colors like crimson ribbons in the darkening sky.

It was the kind of evening for long walks through the park, hand in hand, with that special someone by your side. It was the kind of evening for people in love, people who were meant to be together forever.

Forever.

Deep sadness swelled in her heart again, almost taking her breath away. Without Jared, she would feel sad. Empty. Incomplete.

She grabbed the chain around her neck, forcing herself to remember what he'd done, the way things had to be.

They walked in a silence broken only by the sound of their footsteps crunching on the gravel. Jared suddenly took her hand in his. His strong fingers surrounded hers like a warm glove. Her breath quickened, and before she could pull back or even think clearly, she instinctively curled her hand into his. Her melancholy magically faded away, and she smiled as the breeze blew across her face. And just like that, her heart felt whole again.

But for how long?

*   *   *

Jared led Erin to his favorite spot, situated in the cemetery nestled in the hills high above the city, excited to share it with her. He'd never brought anyone else here, but he wanted to see this with Erin, through her eyes.

He slanted her a glance, smiled and gently squeezed her hand. She nervously pushed her hair behind her ear with her free hand, then ducked her head and gave him one of those shy smiles that always took him out at the knees.

He found the familiar clearing in the foliage on the outskirts of the cemetery. Pulling her tightly next to him, he stopped, shaking off his nervousness about sharing something so personally significant. Deep inside, being here with Erin felt right.

"So." He gestured to the view. "What do you think?"

She gazed out at the stunning vista. "Oh, heavens," she breathed. "It's…beautiful."

The western Portland suburbs fanned out for miles to the west in front of them, until they gave way to thousands of acres of rugged forest land and the Coast Range of mountains, visible in the distance as low-slung, dull-gray smudges against the setting sun. But it was the spectacular sunset that dominated the view. On warm summer nights like this, he'd discovered the sunsets were among the most vivid he'd ever seen.

How many times had he come here long ago to escape one of his father's tirades?

Too many to count.

Old shards of regret and pain cut through him, creating a familiar dull ache in his heart. Without thought, he released Erin's hand and slipped his arm around her shoulder. He dropped his nose to her soft hair, smelling roses and shampoo. A comforting warmth spread through him and the pain within faded.

Relaxing, he gazed westward. "When I was a teenager, I used to ride my bike up here and sit and wait for the sun to set just to see this." He caressed her lower arm with his hand, appreciating the smoothness of her skin.

She turned her head toward him. "You needed to escape."

He raised his brows, surprised yet pleased by her perceptiveness. "Yeah, I did." He smiled and leaned close to her ear. "How did you know that?"

She lifted a slim shoulder. "I had a spot in a nearby park where I always used to go and think when I needed to get away from my mom."

The connection they shared blew him away. They'd both had painful childhoods, ruined by selfish, critical parents. On a deeply personal level she understood the hurt and pain his father had sowed in his son's heart, and understood what haunted him. She could look into his soul and understand him.

Warmth burst in his chest and flooded into his heart. Something important swirled in the back of his brain, something he needed to know....

He stepped back and skimmed his hand down her arm to clasp her hand again. "We need to talk."

She pulled her hand from his and sidled away. "I guess so."

He sensed her withdrawal and it scared him to death. "Do you really think I was trying to buy you off?"

She glared at him, then swung away. "You threw diamonds the size of marbles at me to make me feel better."

"I thought that's what I was supposed to do—"

"Why? Because that's what your father always did?"

He froze, horrified, but knew, deep down, that she'd touched on a painful truth he hadn't been willing to fully see. He'd acted exactly like his father by offering her everything...but his heart.

That knowledge burned like acid inside of him, tightening his throat, momentarily cutting off a coherent reply.

Erin spoke again. "Those earrings reminded me how important it is to keep my heart safe."

"Why?" he managed.

She wrapped her arms around her waist, then turned her leaf-green eyes to him. "Throughout our shaky marriage my ex-husband gave me expensive jewelry to make up for the fact that he was a jerk. He had nothing else to offer me."

"Nothing else," he repeated solemnly, beginning to understand not only Erin, but how he'd let past pain keep him from seeing the truth. He'd wanted her, desired her, and had tried to control her and manipulate their relationship to suit him. But he hadn't ever let himself see the most important thing, what he'd been grasping at all along but had been too stubborn and foolish to figure out.

He loved Erin.

His stomach caved in on itself. Loving her filled him with fear; he was so afraid of paying the price he had always associated with that emotion. But as he looked at Erin standing there, her red-gold hair shaming the vivid sunset painting the sky in front of him, none of that mattered any longer. All that mattered was telling her how he felt.

Filled with blinding, humbling emotion and a newfound sense of purpose, he took her hand and pulled, wanting her to face him when he told her what he'd finally figured out. "Erin, please look at me."

Her chin quivered. Slowly she twisted her head, and her shimmering green gaze met his.

Happiness flooded his being, a happiness so strong and

true he knew everything had to turn out all right. "I love you, Erin. I love you with all my heart."

Her eyes widened, and she jerked away, letting out a sob. "No! Words don't matter when you don't mean them." Huge tears poured down her cheeks. She curled her fingers around that damn chain at her neck, an unmistakable symbol of her inability to let him into her heart.

Her reaction tore a hole in him. He'd hoped his newly discovered love would be enough to break through that wall of hers. But she kept putting up bricks faster than he could take them down. "I wouldn't lie to you. Can't you trust in my love?"

She shakily wiped the tears on her face. "Brent betrayed me and left me with a heart that never healed. Just days ago you thought the worst of me. An *I love you* isn't going to change that."

The slow burn of defeat spread through him. He ignored it and stepped closer, holding on to his last hopes with a death grip. "Don't shut me out, honey. Trust me."

She turned her tear-darkened eyes to him. "No, I can't," she said so softly he could barely hear her. "I can't trust any man ever again. My father left me. Brent left me. And you and the blonde…" She trailed off shaking her head.

"The blonde?"

She bit her lip. "I came to Warfield's the day I lost my job and I saw you and a tall, blond woman together."

He frowned and scanned his memory, then remembered. "That was Nancy Swopes, Dan's wife. He was out sick and she'd come to pick up his paycheck. I've known her forever."

"So she isn't a…girlfriend?"

"Nope."

She stood silently, still chewing on her lip. "Okay. I guess I jumped to the wrong conclusion about her. My mistake. But that doesn't matter enough to make a difference. I just can't snap my fingers and forget that you thought the worst of me," she whispered. "I'm sorry, but I have to go." And then she turned and walked away.

Jared clenched his hands, knowing that despite his overdue discovery he was still losing her with every step she took. Again he wished he could turn back time and fix his mistake. "I'm not Brent," he said loudly, scrabbling for something that would change her mind.

She stopped, her head bent, then turned around. Her tear-stained cheeks and swollen, red eyes stood out starkly against her smooth, pale skin. "No, you're not," she agreed. "But you do remind me of him sometimes." She pressed a stiff hand to her mouth. "I'm sorry."

And with that depressing, painful declaration, she turned away, his heart held in her hands, and left him standing all alone.

With burning eyes he looked at the sunset, hoping to find some kind of comfort. But the sun had already set, leaving nothing but gray clouds and darkness in its wake.

Numb, he roughly repositioned his watch on his arm, then shoved his hands in his pockets and stared at the ground, acknowledging that until a few minutes ago he'd been looking at the situation from the wrong perspective.

His father's perspective.

His thoughts swung to the hard, selfish man who had sired him. Angus Warfield hadn't known love when it bit him in the butt, and he'd lost the one woman who'd loved him despite his crotchety ways.

Jared's mother.

Did he want to end up like his father?

Like a focus button, that simple question put things into instant, perfect perspective. Jared had wanted to avoid his father's mistakes by keeping love out of his heart so he wouldn't be left alone in the end. But his plan had back-fired. He'd ended up exactly how he didn't want to be by trying to avoid what his father had done. But his father's mistake had been to keep his heart closed off, not the opposite.

Jared had been avoiding the wrong mistake all along.

And Erin doubted his love, which nearly killed him. Why had it taken him so long to discover that the only thing that mattered was that he loved Erin James, that the vibrant, wonderful woman she was completed him in a way Allison would never be able to?

Erin might think she could simply walk away, but she was dead wrong. One way or another he would prove to her how foolish she was. He'd make her see what he'd discovered—that past pain and betrayals didn't matter when love was the reward. He'd make her believe. He had to.

As he hurried back to the car to take her home, he refused to consider what he would do if he couldn't.

When Erin shuffled out the next morning, bleary-eyed from lack of sleep, she was surprised to see her mom's small overnight bag sitting at the front door. Oh, please let it be so. She needed a little solitude to nurse her bleeding heart and come to terms with never seeing Jared again.

"Mom?" she called, tightening the belt to her bathrobe around her waist. "Are you leaving?"

Her mom emerged from the small guest bathroom in the hall, her Coral Fantasy lipstick, the same shade she'd worn since the seventies, freshly applied. She pinched her lips together and gave Erin a sour look. "I've done my best to hold my tongue, but I just have to say something now since you were out with that man again last night. What in the world are you thinking? A trash thief?"

Great. Wasn't this just what Erin needed after Jared had told her he loved her and she'd ripped her own heart out and walked away. She'd spent the rest of the night fitfully tossing and turning in agony over her decision.

She was having a major crisis of confidence here.

But she would dutifully tell her mom the truth about Jared to get her off her back and make her happy. She opened her mouth, but the explanation stuck in her throat. She remembered what Jared had said about standing up to her mom. Why should she care what her mom thought when Erin had turned her back on the most wonderful man alive? With that drilling a hole in her heart a mile wide, her mother's opinion seemed pretty insignificant.

And, more important, she'd discovered something last night at the restaurant when she'd demanded that Jared help her out. She'd liked the way she'd felt, the power that had filled her when she stood up for what she wanted, for what she deserved.

She'd discovered that she finally wanted to be able to respect herself. And that meant she couldn't back down now.

Stiffening her shoulders, she fastened a hard expression on her face and said, "Yes, a trash thief. But a good-looking one, don't you think?"

He mother's face turned an unladylike shade of mottled red. "I'm not going to let you screw up your life with some worm-farmer's son. You already ruined your marriage to Brent. I won't let you embarrass me again."

Erin's chest burned. With her heart in tatters and a heady sense of personal power and respect growing inside of her, she wasn't about to take her mother's insults and criticism without firing back some bullets of her own. "Embarrass you? If I want to date the Grinch, I will. Got that?" she snapped.

Her mom stared at her as if she'd sprouted another head, then stalked closer. "Are you talking back to me?"

Feeling stronger than she had in years, Erin stepped forward and met her mother's hard eyes. "Yeah, I am. You say you want to fix things between us, well, let's start now. Butt out."

Her mom's eyes widened. Her mouth worked, but no sound came out. After a long, pregnant pause, she said, "I can't believe it. You've finally stood up for yourself."

Erin dropped her jaw and almost flopped onto the floor in a dead faint. "Ex-ex-excuse me?" Maybe her long, sleepless night had somehow damaged her hearing.

Her mom gave her a quivering half smile and smoothed her serviceable navy-blue skirt. "I've always thought you needed more of a backbone. Good thing you've finally grown one."

Erin stared at her mom. "You…you actually *like* that I'm telling you off?"

Her mom inclined her head. "Well, I can't say that I *like* being told off, but I do admire a woman who stands up for herself, yes."

Erin shook her head and ran a hand through her messy bed-hair. "I guess I should have popped off to you a long time ago, then."

Her mom picked up her sweater and laid it over her arm. "Maybe you should have. I've always been much too tough on you, but seeing you like this makes me think it was all worthwhile. My mother never gave me her opinion on anything. I guess I saw it as my job to do the opposite with you."

Erin pinched her arm to wake herself up. Nothing happened. She wasn't having a strange dream or hadn't landed in some alternate, backward universe. No, this was reality. She shook her head back and forth, stunned that she had come to an understanding of sorts with her mom. Though she doubted they would ever be best friends, it felt good to share one positive thing with her in an otherwise miserable few days.

Her mom opened the door and picked up her bag. "Close your mouth, dear, before your face freezes in that position."

"Mom, wait." Erin held out her hand and walked toward her. "I thought you were staying until tomorrow."

"I was. But you seem to be doing fine—"

"You came here to check on me?"

"Of course I did. You *are* my daughter, you know, and I do care about you. More than you realize, I guess."

An eddy of warmth swirled in Erin's heart, and for the first time in her life she felt that her mom *did* actually love her, even though she showed her love and concern in a weird, sometimes hurtful way. Maybe that was better than a mom who didn't care about her at all.

She squeezed Erin's arm. "Well, I've got to go. And you're right. He's a very good-looking trash thief." She opened the door and stepped outside, then waved with her free hand. "Toodle-oo. Take care."

Rooted to the floor and speechless, Erin waved feebly and watched her breeze out to her car in the driveway.

Before her mom opened the car door, she turned. "Oh, and by the way, some man called last night while you were out and said to tell you that the article you're writing is going to be featured in the Sunday paper. Sounds like your job is going well." She climbed into the car, bag in hand, waved, and slammed the door. She backed out of the driveway and drove away.

A warm, satisfied glow spread through Erin. "The Bachelor Chronicles" follow-up was going to be given a coveted spot in the Sunday paper. Looked like her professional life was back on track again.

Maybe her personal life, too.

It felt really, really good to stand up for herself, discover a grain of her mother's love, and win her grudging approval. Erin had had it in her all along to be strong. With a growing sense of wonder and empowerment she realized that she'd helped perpetuate her mom's negativity by passively accepting her crummy, belittling attitude as something she deserved.

Like a submissive dog, she'd rolled over and taken it. She'd enabled her mom's critical behavior. And—Oh, heavens! She'd done the same thing by meekly standing by and letting Brent treat her like dirt. She hadn't put up a fight or even attempted to take the reins of her life so she could control her own destiny. Feeling weak in the knees, she breathlessly lurched to the couch and sank down onto the soft cushions.

Then, like a bomb, one thought exploded in her head.

I am responsible for my happiness and well-being. Not Brent. Not my mother.

Not Jared.

She had the power to be happy and nobody could take it away from her.

If that were true, maybe she *could* let Jared into her heart. But that thought still terrified her. So much was at stake. Her future. Jared's future. Their happiness.

Everything.

Before she could organize her squirrelly thoughts, a heavy knock sounded on her front door.

Jared's knock.

She froze, a hand pressed to her chest. Her heart pulsed like a trip-hammer. Her nerves pulled taut. Her brain balked, overloaded, confused. Oh, no. She wasn't ready to face him. This was all too new, too fresh, too scary to put to the test.

But she had to face him. Now. She'd learned that she couldn't run away from him, or her feelings, any longer.

And as sure as the knowledge that the sun would set in the west tonight, she knew why Jared was here. They needed to settle this thing between them once and for all.

Okay. Taking a deep, calming breath, she crossed the room on wobbly legs. She paused, her hand on the doorknob. A huge arrow of fear shot through her, but she ignored it. Now wasn't the time to give in to her old, useless insecurities. Now was the time to reach out and grab her happiness by the tail—because she wanted it, deserved it.

She set her jaw and jerked the door open.

Jared stood on her porch, still wearing the clothes he'd had on the night before. He looked like heaven.

A deep, telling happiness blossomed inside of her.

He smiled tentatively, nervously, looking as if he was afraid she was going to slam the door in his face. "Can I come in?"

Not trusting herself to speak, she simply nodded, then stepped aside to let him in. His java scent wafted in behind him, creating a deep, familiar wanting in the pit of her belly. She bit her lip and shut the door.

He didn't waste any time. "I wanted to tell you that you were right last night when you said I was acting like my father." He shook his head and ran a hand through his hair. "I *was* throwing my money around as a substitute for offering up my heart. I'm sorry. You deserve much more."

"Okay," she said neutrally, hoping he would expand on his thoughts.

"I'd always promised myself I wouldn't be like my dad, but in many ways I was, and that really kills me." He rubbed his dark, whisker-shadowed jaw. "It was a lot easier to second-guess our relationship and just…take over than admit to my feelings."

Erin's breath stalled in her chest as she waited for him to finish.

"So, in light of that, I have something to say." He sucked in a huge breath and ceremoniously dropped to one knee.

Erin pressed a trembling hand to her mouth.

He looked at her solemnly. "Erin, I love you, and I can't live without you. You would make me the happiest man on earth if you would marry me." He held a glinting purple object in the air. "Please accept this ring as a token of my undying love."

She frowned and looked at what he held clamped between his fingers. She blinked, then looked again. It was a huge, plastic, purple ring, the kind a little girl would wear with a pink feather boa and her mother's too-big high heels.

A purple, plastic engagement ring?

She yanked her eyebrows together. "What—"

"Let's see if it fits." He grabbed her left hand and pushed the ring to her first knuckle. "Huh. Guess I'll have to have it sized." He eyed the gaudy thing, then grinned up at her. "It looks damn good on you Erin. Purple is definitely your color."

His quick, bright, familiar smile soothed her nervousness and confusion. She let out a tiny laugh, loving this playful side of him. "Where in the world did you get this thing?" She waved her hand in the air.

He stood and lifted one broad shoulder. "Cracker Jacks. Had to look through about a hundred boxes to find the thing."

She laughed again, her mind whirling with excitement. What a crazy way to make a point. But then, that was her Jared. Crazy. "That's a lot of Cracker Jacks."

He took her hand, stroking sparks across her skin. "I'd do it all over again. I love you, and I'd do anything to prove it to you." A deep, true, unmistakable love emanated from his eyes like a candle in the window on a cold, dark night.

A thrill raced through her, and she swallowed past the sudden lump in her throat, hanging on to his gaze with her own. "Oh, Jared..."

He pulled her close and leaned down and gently whispered words across her lips. "Say you love me, Erin. I know you do."

The delicious scent of coffee and cream swirled around her. She sighed as his lips caressed hers, feeling contentment and happiness seep into her, straight from his heart to hers.

She *did* love him.

She'd changed and grown so much, even since last night, when he'd told her he loved her and she hadn't been able to accept his love because of all of the things she was afraid of. Her mom had helped her to understand something that had completed a profound change deep inside of her. She was responsible for her own happiness, no one else.

Letting Jared into her heart was the key to her very own happily-ever-after, especially after he'd proven that he understood her fear of being bought off.

As a calm fell over her, she held out her left hand and looked at her ring. Lord, the thing was ugly, but in a wonderful way. It was the perfect symbol of their love, and it showed her that he not only really loved her but that he understood what had kept her from admitting her love to him.

Jared's love and understanding had healed the wound on her heart.

Tears brimmed in her eyes and fell down her cheeks. "I love you, Jared, and I have for a long time. I was just too afraid to admit it."

His mouth curved into a stunning smile, and his mocha-laced eyes danced with happiness. "Well, it's about time, Ms. James. I thought you'd never realize what a catch I am." He dug into his pants pocket and pulled out a small velvet box. "Now that the pretend ring has done its job, it's time for the real thing." He looked into her eyes and flipped open the box's satin-lined lid. Inside was a sapphire and diamond ring almost identical to the one her father had given her.

Erin's chest burned with the deepest, truest love she'd ever felt. "Oh, Jared," she whispered, pressing a hand to her tight chest. "You remembered." She reached out and took the ring from the box, admiring the deep-blue glow of the round sapphire and the glitter of the small diamonds that encircled it in a gleaming gold-filigree setting.

"Here, let me put it on." He gently removed the purple ring and took the sapphire from her. "I'm sure your father loved you and I do, too. This ring shows how much." He slowly slid the ring onto her left hand.

It fit perfectly. Just like Jared's love.

"I love you," she said, looking into his eyes, finally unafraid to lose herself in his gorgeous coffee gaze. She pulled his mouth down to hers and kissed him long and hard, pressing close, adoring the way they melded perfectly together.

A long time later Jared kissed his way across her cheek and buried his mouth next to her ear. He nibbled, tickling her, then said, "So this bachelor's finally taken?"

"Forever," she said, then kissed him again with every intention of showing him that *this* bachelor's chronicle was a thing of the past.

*   *   *   *   *